JUNIOR GREAT BOOKS

SERIES 3

SECOND SEMESTER

◆ ◆ ◆

AN INTERPRETIVE READING, WRITING, AND DISCUSSION CURRICULUM

JUNIOR GREAT BOOKS

SERIES 3

SECOND SEMESTER

THE GREAT BOOKS FOUNDATION

A nonprofit educational corporation

ISBN 1-880323-03-6

15 14 13 12

Printed in the United States of America

Published and distributed by

THE GREAT BOOKS FOUNDATION
A nonprofit educational corporation

35 East Wacker Drive, Suite 2300

Chicago, IL 60601-2298

CONTENTS

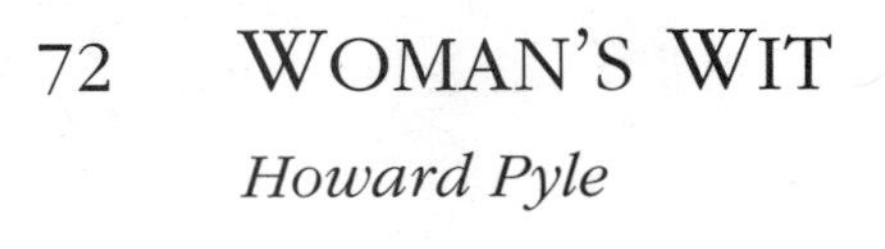

THE BLACK HEART OF INDRI

Dorothy Hoge

In a valley of the hills bordering the province of the Wise Mandarin, Indri had his home. Indri's mother was a water sprite who had been bewitched into marrying a prince of toads and Indri himself had webbed feet and hands and the face of a toad. Perhaps because he was so ugly he also had a black heart.

He lived in a bamboo hut in a deep forest and beside his door ran the stream of the water of life which he had inherited from his father the toad.

•••

Indri sold casks of this water to the people of the valley for as much as he could get, and because they were poor and needed the water so much they were afraid of him.

In his gloomy forest there grew a profusion of beautiful orchids and every day Indri's forest sprites sprinkled them with water from the stream so they never faded. In the center of each bloom a drop of the magic fluid always sparkled. Indri was very proud of his orchids, but still he was unhappy. He sat in his hut and thought how ugly he was.

"What shall I do?" he cried in despair. "I am the saddest creature in the whole world. What good is it to me that my mother is a beautiful water sprite since I have the form of my father the toad? No wonder my heart is black."

Then Indri heard his mother's voice speaking gently. "My son, you only think your heart is black. If you will live for nine days and nights in the presence of virtue, your ugliness will vanish."

This did not help Indri very much for he did not know where to look for virtue.

One day the headman of the village came to Indri's door. His little son lay dying of a strange

•••

illness and the headman was filled with anxiety. "Oh, Indri," he begged, "let me have a cask of your water of life or my boy will die."

Indri was feeling particularly despondent and contrary that day and he answered, "Nam Li, you know my price. Because you are headman, the price is doubled."

Nam Li threw his hands over his head. "True, I am headman. But the money I have spent on my son is beyond reckoning. Not only that, but I am obliged to keep my other children with a relative so the house will be quiet. My wife and I have only a bit of parched rice. I beg you, Indri, have pity on my innocent, virtuous son."

Indri remembered his mother's words and poked his ugly face around the door. "Nam Li, I will give you the water if you will let me

• • •

come and dwell in your home near your son for nine days and nights."

The headman readily consented. He thought he need not look at Indri, and to get the water for nothing was a better bargain than he had hoped for.

Nam Li's son recovered and Indri, who had kept himself out of sight behind the boy's bed and eaten his share of rice in a secluded corner, returned to his forest home full of hope and joy.

But when he looked at himself in his clear stream he found he had not changed a particle. He was enraged.

"I have been fooled," he cried. "There is greed, not virtue in the home of Nam Li." And he shut himself up in his hut and would answer no calls for water from his stream.

Now that his son was well and the remainder of the family had returned home, Nam Li began to think of ways in which he could make money to pay himself back for all the expense of the boy's illness. One night an idea came to him. Calling his two older sons, he led them into the deep forest and they cut all the beautiful orchids

•••

Indri had raised and carried them home in a huge basket. They emptied each flower of the drop of water at its heart until they had a great jar full. This they sold in small quantities to the people of the valley who were glad not to have to go to Indri. As long as the water lasted, the headman made money.

When Indri discovered the loss of his beautiful orchids, he was more furious than ever. "Nam Li is a wicked, ungrateful creature," he stormed as he plunged through the forest. "It is he who deserves to have the head of a toad—or no head at all."

Indri had his forest sprites plant a hedge of thorny mimosa to enclose the forest and the stream of the water of life. Almost overnight it grew thick and impassable and high as a house. The powdery perfume of yellow mimosa blossoms filled the forest. Indri sat in his hut and waited.

After a while the water in the headman's jar gave out. So anxious was Nam Li to make money that he had not saved a drop. Then his little son grew ill again. Immediately Nam Li forgot his greed and aghast at his lack of foresight,

• • •

was willing to offer everything he had for a cask of water from the stream. Knowing how hard it would be to approach Indri after having done him such wrong, he took a few of the townsfolk with him when he went to beg. They stood outside the mimosa hedge and called, but got no answer. Then they wept and wailed and at last Indri came down the overgrown path and looked out over the thorn gate in the hedge and cried in a loud voice to Nam Li. "You evil one, you took my gift of water, you robbed me of my orchids, and sold what did not belong to you. Do you think I am likely to help you now? Go away."

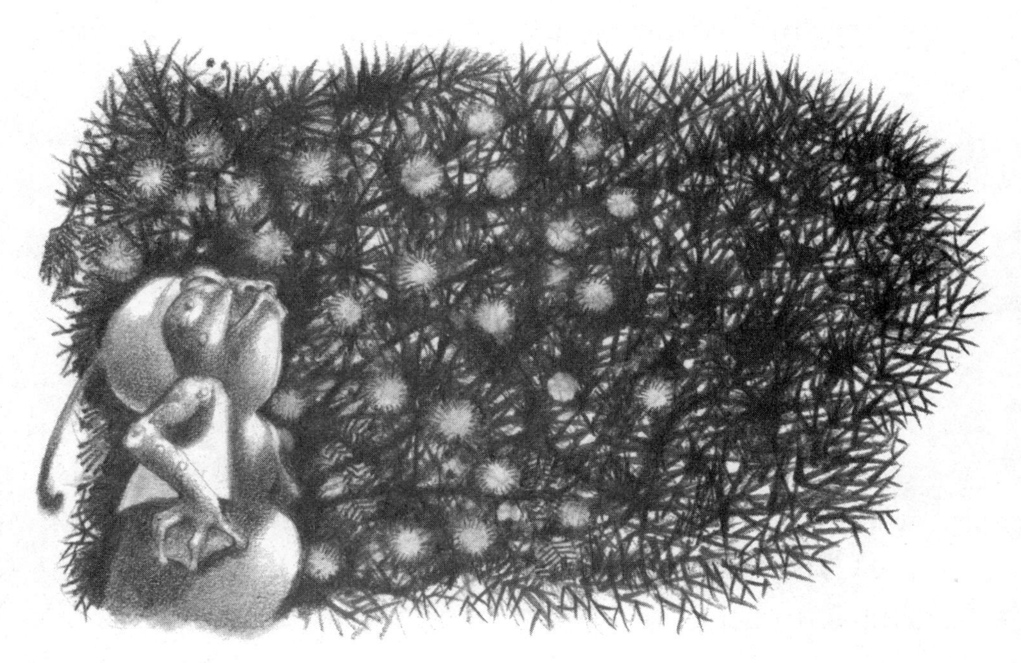

•••

"Oh, Lord Indri," the townsfolk entreated, "think of the life of the little one. Anything the headman has is yours—anything."

"Very well, then," said Indri. "I will take Nam Li's head. Come back to me with his head and I will see if I can spare a little water."

The townsfolk were terribly frightened. Nam Li was thrown into the deepest melancholy. Even if he gave up his head and his child were cured, how would his family be taken care of without him? Finally the townsfolk decided to consult His Excellency the Wise Mandarin, himself. Surely he would not allow their chief to lose his head at the whim of a toad spirit.

So they journeyed through the rice fields and along the dusty roads until they came to the palace and were at last admitted to the august presence of the Mandarin.

He was an imposing figure seated on his lacquer chair. Quilted brocade robes fell about his ample form; his long-nailed hands were folded in gold-embroidered sleeves. He moved scarcely at all as he listened to their story, but his small black eyes were sharp and knowing in his smooth face.

"My friends," he said, "I cannot save your headman. He has brought this on himself through his own greed. He has cheated Indri. I know Indri. He is ugly and his heart is black, but he keeps his word. And in my experience there is always some way to reach a black heart. In finding it, your headman may redeem himself. Go back, and bid him with becoming humility to try again."

The Mandarin closed his eyes and the people knew he had no more to say. They returned downcast because they had already thought of

• • •

every way they knew. Nam Li heard their report in silence. Faced with his son's death and his wife's tears, he could do nothing. In spite of his despair, the headman was brave.

"We will go tonight," he said. "Let my wife think it is a simple journey and when you come back with the water of life you can persuade her that I have met with a man-eating bear, and in her pleasure at saving the child she will forget me. Promise to care for my family and conceal my fate."

The townsfolk promised but they were determined not to slay Nam Li until all else had failed.

Although they were stealthy, one small person had heard them talking and watched them depart. Yua Nana, the headman's little daughter, crept from her couch

◆◆◆

in the dark, resolved to follow and add her entreaties to the townsfolks' in an effort to save her father. The moonlight shimmered upon her hurrying form but her feet were light and made no sound along the road.

Indri, who was waiting in sulky anger to see what would happen next, saw the little group approach his gate. As they came near, he called out, "I don't want your headman. I want his head. Throw me his head and I will throw you a cask of water."

The people drew close and pleaded with him. They offered money, rice fields, all they owned. Indri answered that he had more than enough of everything. All he wanted was Nam Li's head. Finally Nam Li in his wretchedness called out, "Kill me yourself, then, and be done with it."

But Indri shouted back, "I am no executioner. Waste no more time, but throw me his head."

"We will draw lots," said one of the men, "so no one shall have the blame for this dreadful deed."

• • •

While they were hunting twigs of unequal length for the drawing, Yua Nana suddenly appeared and threw herself before her father, her arms about his knees. "Father, Father," she cried in her high, sweet voice. "Indri must not take your life. What would the village and our family do without you? Let him take my head instead, for I am of no consequence to anyone."

The men stopped and looked at her in astonishment. The sound of her sobs came to Indri on the other side of the gate.

"Is she your child?" he asked.

"Yes," said Nam Li.

Yua Nana rose and came close to the gate. "Sir, is there no way I can save my father?"

Indri looked at her beauty in the moonlight and saw the virtue which shone through her tears. "Truly," he said, "I think there is a way." He spoke to Nam Li. "I will make a bargain with you. Leave your daughter with me for nine days and nights. I will do her no harm, but she must come willingly and you must not try to see her. Quickly, now. The girl or your head. I might change my mind."

• • •

Nam Li cried out and tore at his clothes in his misery. "What? Shall I sacrifice my daughter that my little son be saved? No! Take my head."

But Yua Nana, light as a dragonfly, was already through the half-opened gate. Indri tossed a cask of water to the nearest man. In an instant the man set off with it down the road. The thorn gate shut fast, and though Nam Li kicked and shook it, he could not get through. At last he told his friends to leave him and to return at the end of nine days well armed, for if any harm should come to Yua Nana he would kill Indri and burn down the forest.

Indri paid no attention to all this. Inside the mimosa hedge he took Yua Nana gently by the hand. She was weak and frightened. "Lord Indri," she said, "I have come so fast I cannot walk." So Indri lifted her up and carried her in his arms a long way through the forest.

The new orchids he had planted breathed their fragrance on them as they passed, and the dark fingers of the trees reached out and touched them. The moonlight faded and as dawn lit up the forest, they came to the threshold of a fine house. It was approached by a winding path of

•••

gleaming marble guarded by stone lions. Before the doorway was a high screen carved with flowers to keep out the evil spirits. The tiled roof of the house shone gold in the rising sun.

But Yua Nana had fallen asleep. Indri carried her in, laid her on soft cushions, and ordered fine clothes for her and cakes and sweet incense when she should waken.

This was a new world for Yua Nana, and seeing her wonder, Indri outdid himself to

• • •

please her. Every day he brought her presents. He gathered his most beautiful orchids for her, he had the forest birds sing their songs beside the fountain in her honor, and his forest sprites performed such quaint antics for her amusement that they both lost themselves in gaiety and joy. Indri himself even leaped about and made faces just to hear the lovely tinkling sound of her laughter. In fact, he was so taken up with ways to entertain Yua Nana that he completely forgot about his toad features and his black heart.

But when the ninth day arrived he remembered his contract. Indri knew his mother had been mistaken, but now he did not care. He had had more delight than he had ever had in all his lonely life. "Beautiful one," he said sadly to Yua Nana, "the nine days and nights are past. I will go with you as far as my hut and a sprite will conduct you to your father."

Yua Nana put her hand into his webbed fingers. "Dear Indri, I have been so happy here, I cannot bear to go."

"You must go," he answered firmly. "It is the agreement."

• • •

When they arrived at the hut, Indri rushed inside and shut the door and would not even say goodbye. "Mother, Mother, comfort me," he cried. "Yua Nana is gone and your hideous son is left alone in his wretchedness."

His mother's voice replied softly, "My son, he who lives with virtue and makes others happy will never be ugly and alone."

Before Indri could speak, there was a tapping on the door. He rose from his knees and opened it. Yua Nana stood there sadly. "I returned, dear Indri, for I could not go without trying to soothe your sorrow." She lifted her eyes and looked at him and fell back with a cry.

"Oh, my dear!" he exclaimed, "What have I done?"

"I don't know you," she said. "You are so fine, and your face shines with such beauty."

Indri rushed to look at himself and it was indeed true. His figure was straight and handsome, his eyes black and his hair shining. His hands were no longer webbed like a toad's, but smooth and strong. He could hardly speak. "Yua Nana," he said at last, "it is your virtue and love that have released me from the guise of

my father the toad. How can I ever let you go? Without you I shall grow black-hearted again and shall surely die."

She took his smooth fingers in her own. "Let us go together to my father."

When they reached the thorn gate in the mimosa hedge they found Nam Li, weak and pale from anxiety, waiting for them. But as they approached, the headman saw his daughter's happy face and the fine young man walking beside her and he was astonished. When he had heard their story he made a deep bow.

• • •

"My Lord Indri," he said, "truly our great Mandarin is full of wisdom. He knew there was a way to touch your heart, but it was my virtuous daughter, not my unworthy self, who found it. I beg forgiveness for my greed."

"I, too, ask forgiveness," replied Indri, "for my hard heart. Hereafter the path through the forest shall be kept cleared and the water of life from my stream shall be free for the use of all

◆◆◆

who need it. If I may have Yua Nana for my bride, I shall ask for nothing else."

Nam Li was delighted at such a fine prospect, but he considered a moment. "If you want Yua Nana would it not be wise to let me sell the water for you until you get enough money to build a house fit for her to live in?"

Indri laughed as he clasped Yua Nana's hand in his. "Watch your head, headman and august father-in-law. I already have all I need, as I told you before. It is said by the wise ones that greed is at the base of all evil. As for the water of life, happy are they who shall drink of it and never grow old, for their love shall last forever."

THE GREEN MAN

Gail E. Haley

The story you are about to read may have happened just this way—or perhaps it came about in a different manner in some other place entirely. . . .

Claude was the only son of Squire Archibald. He was arrogant, vain, and selfish. He spent most of his time hunting, hawking, and riding about the countryside in his fine clothes.

One evening Claude rode into the village, and after ordering a lavish meal at The Mermaid and Bush, he sat watching the bustle of village life.

•••

"Look at those ignorant peasants putting food out for the Green Man when they can barely feed their own children."

"They are grateful, Master Claude," replied the landlord. "For the Green Man keeps their animals healthy. He protects their children if they stray into the forest. Without him, the crops would not grow, nor the seasons turn in their course."

"Rubbish! Those are just silly tales. There is no Green Man!"

"Mind your tongue, sir," chided the landlord. "Terrible things can happen to those who make fun of old beliefs."

Some days afterward, Claude set out for a day's hunting. He never hunted on foot; he preferred to shoot from horseback. His men and dogs had gone ahead as beaters to drive the game toward him, but nothing was happening, and Claude grew tired of waiting. He rode deeper into the forest.

•••

"Those beaters are incompetent. I haven't seen an animal all day!" he grumbled.

Soon Claude was hopelessly lost. It was hot, and his clothes felt heavy, when through the trees he saw a shady pond. Tethering his horse to a tree, he stripped off his clothes and dived into the cool water. He did not see a thin bony hand reaching out of the bushes.

Claude came out of the water refreshed and hungry, but on the bank he found nothing but a coil of rope.

Claude tied some leafy branches around his waist with the rope. Then he ate some of the strawberries that were growing on the bank. Feeling better, he chose a stout branch as a walking stick and set off to find his way home. But as the day drew to a close, Claude realized that he would have to spend the night in the forest.

Peering about in the gloom, he saw before him the entrance to a large cave and felt his way inside. As he grew accustomed to the dark, Claude realized that he was not alone. There seemed to be something with glittering eyes and sharp horns near the mouth of the cave.

◆◆◆

"Stay back! I'm armed!" Claude shouted. But the creature came no closer. Then something moved near the back of the cave. Claude clutched his stick for protection and drew his legs up onto a ledge. He lay there until, exhausted, he fell asleep.

When Claude woke it was morning and a little nanny goat was standing before him, tossing her head. He laughed with relief. It must have been she who had been at the back of the cave in the night.

•••

Claude looked around. A young rooster was pecking busily near a nest full of eggs. A clay jug and a stone ax hung on the wall above Claude's head. Several rough baskets stood on the floor, and there was ash from a recent fire.

"“This is someone's home,” thought Claude. “Perhaps I should feed the animals.” He gave the hens some grain which he found in a bowl and picked some fresh grass for the goat as a special treat. Then he helped himself to goat's milk and eggs.

The goat nuzzled his hand, and he scratched her behind the ears. She frisked about and followed him when he set off to explore.

Not far away, Claude found a bees' nest in a tree, its honeycomb shining from inside the hollow trunk. Covering his body with mud to protect himself from stings, he climbed up to collect some honey.

Just then, a party of his father's men broke through the trees, blowing their horns and hallooing for him.

“They'll think I've gone mad, if they see me sitting in a tree covered with mud,” thought Claude. “I can't let them see me without my clothes and my boots. I would be disgraced!”

So he let the party pass without revealing himself. Then he climbed down from the tree and crept back to the cave, followed all the time by the goat.

"I'll borrow something to cover myself from the owner of the cave when he returns, and then I'll set off for home again," Claude said to his new friend, the goat. But time passed, and no one came. Claude lived on in the cave, growing leaner and stronger every day.

• • •

As the warm days went by, Claude forgot altogether about clothes. He nearly forgot that he was Claude, the Squire's son. He became Milker-of-the-Goat, Feeder-of-the-Hens, Friend-of-All-Wild-Animals. The forest creatures were not afraid of him. He fed them, talked to them, and spent hours watching them hunt and play.

As the berries, fruits, and nuts ripened, Claude became Gatherer-and-Preserver. When the grain was harvested in distant fields, he became Gleaner, venturing out at night to gather the leftovers for himself and his animals.

Claude was enjoying his new life. Even the sun and the moon seemed to smile upon him.

One morning, after a heavy rainstorm, Claude heard a frantic bellow coming from the direction of the river. He hurried there to see what was wrong, and found a cow who had been separated from her calf. They had taken shelter from the rain in a hilltop thicket, and as the water rose the river had surrounded them,

•••

turning the hillock into an island. The terrified calf would not follow its mother through the swirling current, and the cow was mooing loudly for help.

Claude waded across the water, picked up the calf, and carried it to its mother. Gratefully, the cow licked his hand and then led her calf away through the forest toward the safety of the farmyard.

As the days grew colder, Claude added more ivy leaves to his costume. He tucked strips of moss and lichen between them to keep out the cold. He pounded birch bark to make it soft, and sewed pieces together to make a curtain for the mouth of the cave. After several attempts he even succeeded in making himself some birch-bark boots.

He built a fireplace near the entrance. He had found stones the right size and shape to make a mortar and a pestle, and each day he ground grain or nuts or acorns into flour. The smell of baking bread filled the air. A family of hedgehogs moved in.

The cave was now well stocked with food. Strings of mushrooms, parsnips, wild onions, and herbs hung on drying poles. Claude made slings for the fruit and vegetables he had gathered. He formed barrels out of bark to hold apples and roots. Baskets of nuts, grain, and seeds were stored on a shelf above his mossy bed.

One day when Claude was out gathering acorns, he encountered a fierce wild boar threatening two small children from the village.

"Don't be such a selfish swine!" Claude spoke firmly to the boar. "There are enough acorns for everyone. Go away and let the children have their share."

The boar snorted defiantly but turned and trotted back into the forest.

◆◆◆

"There, there, don't cry. The old boar is gone now," Claude comforted the children.

The girl looked up through her tears at the tall, sunburned man. He seemed as ancient, green, and moss-covered as the oak tree that towered above them.

"Are you the Green Man?" she asked in a whisper.

Claude looked down in surprise. Warm sunshine caressed his hair. A gentle breeze rippled his leafy costume. His feet felt as if they were rooted in the earth.

"Yes," Claude answered her at last, "I am the Green Man."

He helped the children to gather up their acorns and filled their basket to the brim. Then he led them safely to the edge of the forest.

• • •

When winter came, at night Claude visited the nearby sleeping villages. He helped himself to some of the food put out for him but always left some for hungry, prowling animals. At times he felt lonely as he walked through the deserted streets, looking into the windows of the cozy houses. He was homesick for his own village and his family. But he returned each night to his cave and his animals. He was needed now in the forest.

Winter passed and spring was on its way. The smell of budding leaves, warm earth, and growing things filled the air. The days went by, and when he knew that the strawberries would be ripening by the pond, Claude went to pick them.

A man was splashing in the water. A fine suit of clothing lay on the bank and a handsome horse was tethered nearby.

Claude quietly took off his leaves and put on the clothes. He found shears and a glass in the horse's saddlebag, so he cut his long hair and trimmed his beard. Then he rode through the forest until he found his own home.

***

His mother and father were amazed and delighted to see him. Everyone thought that he had been killed long ago by robbers or eaten by wild animals.

"It was the Green Man who saved my life," was all that Claude would say.

His year away had changed the arrogant young man. Now he was hospitable to travelers. He cared for his animals. And each night Claude set out food and drink for the Green Man.

"What is fly?" asked the mousewife.

THE MOUSEWIFE

Rumer Godden

Wherever there is an old house with wooden floors and beams and rafters and wooden stairs and wainscots and skirting boards and larders, there are mice. They creep out on the carpets for crumbs, they whisk in and out of their holes, they run in the wainscot and between the ceiling and the floors. There are no signposts because they know the way, and no milestones because no one is there to see how they run.

In the old nursery rhyme, when the cat went to see the queen, he caught a little mouse under her chair; that was long long ago and

• • •

that queen was different from our queen, but the mouse was the same.

Mice have always been the same. There are no fashions in mice, they do not change. If a mouse could have a portrait painted of his great-great-grandfather, and *his* great-grandfather, it would be the portrait of a mouse today.

But once there was a little mousewife who was different from the rest.

She looked the same; she had the same ears and prick nose and whiskers and dewdrop eyes; the same little bones and grey fur; the same skinny paws and long skinny tail.

•••

She did all the things a mousewife does: she made a nest for the mouse babies she hoped to have one day; she collected crumbs of food for her husband and herself; once she bit the tops off a whole bowl of crocuses; and she played with the other mice at midnight on the attic floor.

"What more do you want?" asked her husband.

She did not know what it was she wanted, but she wanted more.

The house where these mice lived belonged to a spinster lady called Miss Barbara Wilkinson. The mice thought the house was the whole world. The garden and the wood that lay round it were as far away to them as the stars are to you, but the mousewife used sometimes to creep up on the window sill and press her whiskers close against the pane.

In spring she saw snowdrops and appleblossom in the garden and bluebells in the wood; in summer there were roses; in autumn all the trees changed colour; and in winter they were bare until the snow came and they were white with snow.

The mousewife saw all these through the windowpane, but she did not know what they were.

She was a house mouse, not a garden mouse or a field mouse; she could not go outside.

"I think about cheese," said her husband. "Why don't you think about cheese?"

Then, at Christmas, he had an attack of indigestion through eating rich crumbs of Christmas cake. "There were currants in those crumbs," said the mousewife. "They have upset you. You must go to bed and be kept warm." She decided to move the mousehole to a space behind the fender where it was warm. She lined the new hole with tufts of carpet wool and

• • •

put her husband to bed wrapped in a pattern of grey flannel that Miss Wilkinson's lazy maid, Flora, had left in the dustpan. "But I am grateful to Flora," said the mousewife's husband as he settled himself comfortably in bed.

Now the mousewife had to find all the food for the family in addition to keeping the hole swept and clean.

She had no time for thinking.

While she was busy, a boy brought a dove to Miss Wilkinson. He had caught it in the wood. It was a pretty thing, a turtledove. Miss Wilkinson put it in a cage on the ledge of her sitting-room window.

The cage was an elegant one; it had gilt bars and a door that opened if its catch were pressed down; there were small gilt trays for water and peas. Miss Wilkinson hung up a lump of sugar and a piece of fat. "There, you have everything you want," said Miss Barbara Wilkinson.

For a day or two the dove pecked at the bars and opened and shut its wings. Sometimes it called "Roo coo, roo coo," then it was silent.

"Why won't it eat?" asked Miss Barbara Wilkinson. "Those are the very best peas."

•••

A mouse family seldom has enough to eat. It is difficult to come by crumbs, especially in such a neat, tidy house as Miss Barbara Wilkinson's. It was the peas that first attracted the attention of the mousewife to the cage when at last she had time to go up on the window sill. "I have been running here and there and everywhere to get us food," she said, "not allowing myself to come up onto the window sill, and here are these fine white peas, not to mention this piece of fat." (She did not care for the sugar.)

She squeezed through the bars of the cage but, as she was taking the first pea from the tray, the dove moved its wings. I cannot tell you

•••

how quickly the mousewife pressed herself back through the bars and jumped down from the sill and ran across the floor and whisked into her hole. It was quicker than a cat can wink its eye. (She thought it was the cat.)

In spite of her great fright she could not help thinking of those peas. She was very hungry.

"I had better not go back," she said. "There is something dangerous there," but back she went the very next day.

Soon the dove grew quite used to the mousewife going in and out, and the mouse grew quite used to the dove.

"This is better," said Miss Barbara Wilkinson. "The dove is eating its peas," but, of course, he was not; it was the mouse.

The dove kept his wings folded. The mousewife thought him large and strange and ugly with the speckles on his breast and his fine down. (She thought of it as fur, not feathers.) He was not at all like a mouse; his voice was deep and soft, quite unlike hers, which was a small, high squeaking. Most strange of all, to her, was that he let her take his peas; when she offered them to him he turned his head aside on his breast.

•••

"Then at least take a little water," begged the mousewife, but he said he did not like water. "Only dew, dew, dew," he said.

"What is dew?" asked the mousewife.

He could not tell her what dew was, but he told her how it shines on the leaves and grass in the early morning for doves to drink. That made him think of night in the woods and of how he and his mate would come down with the first light to walk on the wet earth and peck for food, and of how, then, they would fly over the fields to other woods farther away. He told this to the mousewife too.

"What is fly?" asked the ignorant little mousewife.

"Don't you know?" asked the dove in surprise. He stretched out his wings and they hit the cage bars. Still he struggled to spread them, but the bars were too close, and he sank back on his perch and sank his head on his breast.

The mousewife was strangely moved but she did not know why.

Because he would not eat his peas she brought him crumbs of bread and, once, a preserved blackberry that had fallen from

a tart. (But he would not eat the blackberry.) Every day he talked to her about the world outside the window.

He told her of roofs and the tops of trees and of the rounded shapes of hills and the flat look of fields and of the mountains far away. "But I have never flown as far as that," he said, and he was quiet. He was thinking now he never would.

To cheer him the mousewife asked him to tell her about the wind; she heard it in the house on stormy nights, shaking the doors and windows with more noise than all the mice put together. The dove told her how it blew in the cornfields, making patterns in the corn,

• • •

and of how it made different sounds in the different sorts of trees, and of how it blew up the clouds and sent them across the sky.

He told her these things as a dove would see them, as it flew, and the mousewife, who was used to creeping, felt her head growing dizzy as if she were spinning on her tail, but all she said was, "Tell me more."

Each day the dove told her more. When she came he would lift his head and call to her, "Roo coo, roo coo," in his most gentle voice.

"Why do you spend so much time on the window sill?" asked her husband. "I do not like it. The proper place for a mousewife is in her hole or coming out for crumbs and frolic with me."

The mousewife did not answer. She looked far away.

Then, on a happy day, she had a nestful of baby mice. They were not as big as half your thumb, and they were pink and hairless, with pink shut eyes and little pink tails like threads. The mousewife loved them very much. The eldest, who was a girl, she called Flannelette, after the pattern of grey flannel.

For several days she thought of nothing and no one else. She was also busy with her husband. His digestion was no better.

One afternoon he went over to the opposite wall to see a friend. He was well enough to do that, he said, but certainly not well enough to go out and look for crumbs. The mice-babies were asleep, the hole was quiet, and the mousewife began to think of the dove. Presently she tucked the nest up carefully and went up on the window sill to see him; also she was hungry and needed some peas.

What a state he was in! He was drooping and nearly exhausted because he had eaten scarcely

• • •

anything while she had been away. He cowered over her with his wings and kissed her with his beak; she had not known his feathers were so soft or that his breast was so warm. "I thought you had gone, gone, gone," he said over and over again.

"Tut! Tut!" said the mousewife. "A body has other things to do. I can't be always running off to you." But, though she pretended to scold him, she had a tear at the end of her whisker for the poor dove. (Mouse tears look like millet seeds, which are the smallest seeds I know.)

She stayed a long time with the dove. When she went home, I am sorry to say, her husband bit her on the ear.

That night she lay awake thinking of the dove; mice stay up a great part of the night, but, towards dawn, they, too, curl into their beds and sleep. The mousewife could not sleep. She still thought of the dove. "I cannot visit him as much as I could wish," she said. "There is my husband, and he has never bitten me before. There are the children, and it is surprising how quickly crumbs are eaten up. And no one would believe how dirty a hole can get if it is not attended to every day. But that is not the worst of it. The dove should not be in that cage. It is thoughtless of Miss Barbara Wilkinson." She grew angry as she thought of it. "Not to be able to scamper about the floor! Not to be able to run in and out, or climb up the larder to get at the cheese! Not to flick in and out and to whisk and to feel how you run in your tail! To sit in the trap until your little bones are stiff and your whiskers grow stupid because there is nothing for them to smell or hear or see!" The mousewife could only think of it as a mouse, but she could feel as the dove could feel.

Her husband and Flannelette and the other children were breathing and squeaking happily in their sleep, but the mousewife could hear her heart beating; the beats were little, like the tick of a watch, but they felt loud and disturbing to her. "I cannot sleep," said the mousewife, and then, suddenly, she felt she must go then, that minute, to the dove. "It is too late. He will be asleep," she said, but still she felt she should go.

She crept from her bed and out of the hole onto the floor by the fender. It was bright moonlight, so bright that it made her blink.

◆◆◆

It was bright as day, but a strange day, that made her head swim and her tail tremble. Her whiskers quivered this way and that, but there was no one and nothing to be seen; no sound, no movement anywhere.

She crept across the pattern of the carpet, stopping here and there on a rose or a leaf or on the scroll of the border. At last she reached the wall and ran lightly up onto the window sill and looked into the cage. In the moonlight she could see the dove sleeping in his feathers, which were ruffled up so that he looked plump and peaceful, but, as she watched, he dreamed

• • •

and called "roo coo" in his sleep and shivered as if he moved. "He is dreaming of scampering and running free," said the mousewife. "Poor thing! Poor dove!"

She looked out into the garden. It too was as bright as day, but the same strange day. She could see the tops of the trees in the wood, and she knew, all at once, that was where the dove should be, in the trees and the garden and the wood.

He called "roo coo" again in his sleep—and she saw that the window was open.

Her whiskers grew still and then they stiffened. She thought of the catch on the cage door. If the catch were pressed down, the door opened.

"I shall open it," said the mousewife. "I shall jump on it and hang from it and swing from it, and it will be pressed down; the door will open and the dove can come out. He can whisk quite out of sight. Miss Barbara Wilkinson will not be able to catch him."

She jumped at the cage and caught the catch in her strong little teeth and swung. The door sprang open, waking the dove.

He was startled and lifted his wings and they hit hard against the cage so that it shivered and the mousewife was almost shaken off.

"Hurry! Hurry!" she said through her teeth.

In a heavy sidelong way he sidled to the door and stood there looking. The mousewife would have given him a push, but she was holding down the catch.

At the door of the cage the dove stretched his neck towards the open window. "Why does he not hurry?" thought the mousewife. "I cannot stay here much longer. My teeth are cracking."

He did not see her or look towards her; then—clap—he took her breath away so that she

• • •

fell. He had opened his wings and flown straight out. For a moment he dipped as if he would fall, his wings were cramped, and then he moved them and lifted up and up and flew away across the tops of the trees.

The mousewife picked herself up and shook out her bones and her fur.

"So that is to fly," she said. "Now I know." She stood looking out of the window where the dove had gone.

"He has flown," she said. "Now there is no one to tell me about the hills and the corn and the clouds. I shall forget them. How shall I remember when there is no one to tell me and there are so many children and crumbs and bits of fluff to think of?" She had millet tears, not on her whiskers but in her eyes.

"Tut! tut!" said the mousewife and blinked them away. She looked out again and saw the stars.

It has been given to few mice to see the stars; so rare is it that the mousewife had not even heard of them, and when she saw them shining she thought at first they must be new brass buttons. Then she saw they were very far off,

farther than the garden or the wood, beyond the farthest trees. "But not too far for me to see," she said. She knew now that they were not buttons but something far and big and strange. "But not so strange to me," she said, "for I have seen them. And I have seen them for myself," said the mousewife, "without the dove. I can see for myself," said the mousewife, and slowly, proudly, she walked back to bed.

She was back in the hole before her husband waked up, and he did not know that she had been away.

Miss Barbara Wilkinson was astonished to find the cage empty next morning and the dove gone. "Who could have let it out?" asked

• • •

Miss Wilkinson. She suspected Flora and never knew that she was looking at someone too large and that it was a very small person indeed.

The mousewife is a very old lady mouse now. Her whiskers are grey and she cannot scamper anymore; even her running is slow. But her great-great-grandchildren, the children of the children of the children of Flannelette and Flannelette's brothers and sisters, treat her with the utmost respect.

She is a little different from them, though she looks the same. I think she knows something they do not.

The wind swept bitterly across the peak.

THE FIRE ON THE MOUNTAIN

Ethiopian folktale as told by
Harold Courlander and Wolf Leslau

People say that in the old days in the city of Addis Ababa there was a young man by the name of Arha. He had come as a boy from the country of Guragé, and in the city he became the servant of a rich merchant, Haptom Hasei.

Haptom Hasei was so rich that he owned everything that money could buy, and often he was very bored because he had tired of everything he knew, and there was nothing new for him to do.

One cold night, when the damp wind was blowing across the plateau, Haptom called

to Arha to bring wood for the fire. When Arha was finished, Haptom began to talk.

"How much cold can a man stand?" he said, speaking at first to himself. "I wonder if it would be possible for a man to stand on the highest peak, Mount Sululta, where the coldest winds blow, through an entire night, without blankets or clothing, and yet not die?"

"I don't know," Arha said. "But wouldn't it be a foolish thing?"

"Perhaps, if he had nothing to gain by it, it would be a foolish thing to spend the night that way," Haptom said. "But I would be willing to bet that a man couldn't do it."

"I am sure a courageous man could stand naked on Mount Sululta throughout an entire night and not die of it," Arha said. "But as for me, it isn't my affair since I've nothing to bet."

"Well, I'll tell you what," Haptom said. "Since you are so sure it can be done, I'll make a bet with you anyway. If you can stand among the rocks on Mount Sululta for an entire night, without food or water or clothing or blankets or fire, and not die of it, then I will give you

• • •

ten acres of good farmland for your own, with a house and cattle."

Arha could hardly believe what he had heard.

"Do you really mean this?" he asked.

"I am a man of my word," Haptom replied.

"Then tomorrow night I will do it," Arha said, "and afterwards, for all the years to come, I shall till my own soil."

But he was very worried, because the wind swept bitterly across the peak. So in the morning Arha went to a wise old man from the Guragé tribe and told him of the bet he had made. The old man listened quietly and thoughtfully, and when Arha had finished he said:

"I will help you. Across the valley from Sululta is a high rock which can be seen in the daytime. Tomorrow night, as the sun goes down, I shall build a fire there, so that it can be seen from where you stand on the peak. All night long you must watch the light of my fire. Do not close your eyes or let the darkness creep upon you. As you watch my fire, think of its warmth, and think of me, your friend, sitting there tending it for you. If you do this, you will survive, no matter how bitter the night wind."

Arha thanked the old man warmly and went back to Haptom's house with a light heart. He told Haptom he was ready, and in the afternoon Haptom sent him, under the watchful eyes of other servants, to the top of Mount Sululta. There, as night fell, Arha removed his clothes and stood in the damp cold wind that swept across the plateau with the setting sun. Across the valley, several miles away, Arha saw the light of his friend's fire, which shone like a star in the blackness.

The wind turned colder and seemed to pass through his flesh and chill the marrow in his bones. The rock on which he stood felt like ice. Each hour the cold numbed him more, until he thought he would never be warm again, but he kept his eyes upon the twinkling light across the valley and remembered that his old friend sat there tending a fire for him. Sometimes wisps of fog passed. He sneezed and coughed and

•••

shivered and began to feel ill. Yet all night through he stood there, and only when the dawn came did he put on his clothes and go down the mountain back to Addis Ababa.

Haptom was very surprised to see Arha, and he questioned his servants thoroughly.

"Did he stay all night without food or drink or blankets or clothing?"

"Yes," his servants said. "He did all of these things."

• • •

"Well, you are a strong fellow," Haptom said to Arha. "How did you manage to do it?"

"I simply watched the light of a fire on a distant hill," Arha said.

"What! You watched a fire? Then you lose the bet, and you are still my servant, and you own no land!"

"But this fire was not close enough to warm me, it was far across the valley!"

"I won't give you the land," Haptom said. "You didn't fulfill the conditions. It was only the fire that saved you."

Arha was very sad. He went again to his friend of the Guragé tribe and told him what had happened.

"Take the matter to the judge," the old man advised him.

Arha went to the judge and complained, and the judge sent for Haptom. When Haptom told his story, and the servants said once more that Arha had watched a distant fire across the valley, the judge said:

"No, you have lost, for Haptom Hasei's condition was that you must be without fire."

Once more Arha went to his old friend with the sad news that he was doomed to the life of a servant, as though he had not gone through the ordeal on the mountaintop.

"Don't give up hope," the old man said. "More wisdom grows wild in the hills than in any city judge."

He got up from where he sat and went to find a man named Hailu, in whose house he had been a servant when he was young.

• • •

He explained to the good man about the bet between Haptom and Arha, and asked if something couldn't be done.

"Don't worry about it," Hailu said after thinking for a while. "I will take care of it for you."

Some days later Hailu sent invitations to many people in the city to come to a feast at his house. Haptom was among them, and so was the judge who had ruled Arha had lost the bet.

When the day of the feast arrived, the guests came riding on mules with fine trappings, their servants strung out behind them on foot. Haptom came with twenty servants, one of whom held a silk umbrella over his head to shade him from the sun, and four drummers played music that signified the great Haptom was here.

The guests sat on soft rugs laid out for them and talked. From the kitchen came the odors of wonderful things to eat: roast goat, roast corn and durra, pancakes called injera, and many tantalizing sauces. The smell of the food only accentuated the hunger of the guests. Time passed. The food should have been served,

but they didn't see it, only smelled vapors that drifted from the kitchen. The evening came, and still no food was served. The guests began to whisper among themselves. It was very curious that the honorable Hailu had not had the food brought out. Still the smells came from the kitchen. At last one of the guests spoke out for all the others:

"Hailu, why do you do this to us? Why do you invite us to a feast and then serve us nothing?"

"Why, can't you smell the food?" Hailu asked with surprise.

"Indeed we can, but smelling is not eating, there is no nourishment in it!"

"And is there warmth in a fire so distant that it can hardly be seen?" Hailu asked. "If Arha was warmed by the fire he watched while standing on Mount Sululta, then you have been fed by the smells coming from my kitchen."

•••

The people agreed with him; the judge now saw his mistake, and Haptom was shamed. He thanked Hailu for his advice, and announced that Arha was then and there the owner of the land, the house, and the cattle.

Then Hailu ordered the food brought in, and the feast began.

WOMAN'S WIT

Howard Pyle

In the days when the great and wise King Solomon lived and ruled, evil spirits and demons were as plentiful in the world as wasps in summer.

So King Solomon, who was so wise and knew so many potent spells that he had power over evil such as no man has had before or since, set himself to work to put those enemies of mankind out of the way. Some he conjured into bottles and sank into the depths of the sea; some he buried in the earth; some he destroyed altogether, as one burns hair in a candle flame.

•••

Now, one pleasant day when King Solomon was walking in his garden with his hands behind his back, and his thoughts busy as bees with this or that, he came face to face with a Demon who was a prince of his kind. "Ho, little man!" cried the evil spirit, in a loud voice. "Art not thou the wise King Solomon who conjures my brethren into brass chests and glass bottles? Come, try a fall at wrestling with me, and whoever conquers shall be master over the other for all time. What do you say to such an offer as that?"

"I say aye!" said King Solomon, and, without another word, he stripped off his royal robes and stood bare-breasted, man to man with the other.

The world never saw the like of that wrestling match between the King and the Demon, for they struggled and strove together from the seventh hour in the morning to the sunset in the evening, and during that time the sky was clouded over as black as night, and the lightning forked and shot, and the thunder roared and bellowed, and the earth shook and quaked.

•••

But at last the King gave the enemy an under twist, and flung him down on the earth so hard that the apples fell from the trees; and then, panting and straining, he held the evil one down, knee on neck. Thereupon the sky presently cleared again, and all was as pleasant as a spring day.

King Solomon bound the Demon with spells, and made him serve him for seven years. First, he had him build a splendid palace, the like of which was not to be seen within the bounds of the seven rivers; then he made him set around the palace a garden, such as I for one wish I may see some time or other. Then, when the Demon had done all that the King wished, the King conjured him into a bottle, corked it tightly, and set the royal seal on the stopper. Then he took the bottle a thousand miles away into the wilderness, and, when no man was looking, buried it in the ground, and this is the way the story begins.

• • •

Well, the years came and the years went, and the world grew older and older, and kept changing (as all things do but two), so that by-and-by the wilderness where King Solomon had hid the bottle became a great town, with people coming and going, and all as busy as bees about their own business and other folk's affairs.

Among these townspeople was a little Tailor, who made clothes for many a worse man to wear, and who lived all alone in a little house with no one to darn his stockings for him, and no one to meddle with his coming and going, for he was a bachelor.

The little Tailor was a thrifty soul, and by hook and crook had laid by enough money to fill a small pot, and then he had to bethink himself of some safe place to hide it. So one night he took a spade and a lamp and went out in the garden to bury his money. He drove his spade into the ground—and click! He struck something hard that rang under his foot with a sound as of iron. "Hello!" said he. "What have we here?" And if he had known as much as you and I do, he would have filled in the earth, and tramped it down, and have left that plate of broth for somebody else to burn his mouth with.

As it was, he scraped away the soil, and then he found a box of adamant, with a ring in the lid to lift it by. The Tailor clutched the ring and bent his back, and up came the box with the damp earth sticking to it. He cleaned the mold away, and there he saw, written in red letters, these words:

"Open not."

You may be sure that after he had read these words he was not long in breaking open the lid of the box with his spade.

Inside the first box he found a second, and upon it the same words:

"Open not."

• • •

Within the second box was another, and within that still another, until there were seven in all, and on each were written the same words:

"Open not."

Inside the seventh box was a roll of linen, and inside that a bottle filled with nothing but blue smoke; and I wish that bottle had burned the Tailor's fingers when he touched it.

"And is this all?" said the little Tailor, turning the bottle upside down and shaking it, and peeping at it by the light of the lamp. "Well, since I have gone so far I might as well open it, as I have already opened the seven boxes." Thereupon he broke the seal that stoppered it.

Pop! Out flew the cork, and—Puff! Out came the smoke; not all at once, but in a long thread that rose up as high as the stars, and then spread until it hid their light.

The Tailor stared and goggled and gaped to see so much smoke come out of such a little bottle, and, as he goggled and stared, the smoke began to gather together again, thicker and thicker, and darker and darker, until it was as black as ink. Then out from it there stepped

one with eyes that shone like sparks of fire, and who had a countenance so terrible that the Tailor's skin quivered and shrivelled, and his tongue clove to the roof of his mouth at the sight of it.

"Who are thou?" said the terrible being, in a voice that made the very marrow of the poor Tailor's bones turn soft from terror.

"If you please, sir," said he, "I am only a little Tailor."

The evil being lifted up both hands and eyes. "How wonderful," he cried, "that one little Tailor can undo in a moment that which took the wise Solomon a whole day to accomplish,

• • •

and in the doing of which he well-nigh broke the sinews of his heart!" Then, turning to the Tailor, who stood trembling like a rabbit, "Hark thee!" said he. "For two thousand years I lay there in that bottle, and no one came nigh to aid me. Thou hast liberated me, and thou shalt not go unrewarded. Every morning at the seventh hour I will come to thee, and I will perform for thee whatever task thou mayest command me. But there is one condition attached to the agreement, and woe be to thee if that condition is broken. If any morning I should come to thee, and thou hast no task for me to do, I shall wring thy neck as thou mightest wring the neck of a sparrow." Thereupon he was gone in an instant, leaving the little Tailor half dead with terror.

Now it happened that the prime minister of that country had left an order with the Tailor for a suit of clothes, so the next morning, when the Demon came, the little man set him to work on the bench, with his legs tucked up like a journeyman tailor. "I want," said he, "such and such a suit of clothes."

"You shall have them," said the Demon; and thereupon he began snipping in the air

• • •

and cutting most wonderful patterns of silks and satins out of nothing at all, and the little Tailor sat and gaped and stared. Then the Demon began to drive the needle like a spark of fire—the like was never seen in all the seven Kingdoms, for the clothes seemed to make themselves.

At last, at the end of a little while, the Demon stood up and brushed his hands. "They are done," said he, and thereupon he instantly vanished. But the Tailor cared little for that, for upon the bench there lay such a suit of clothes of silk and satin stuff, sewed with threads of gold and silver and set with jewels, as the eyes of

•••

man never saw before; and the Tailor packed them up and marched off with them himself to the prime minister.

The prime minister wore the clothes to court that very day, and before evening they were the talk of the town. All the world ran to the Tailor and ordered clothes of him, and his fortune was made. Every day the Demon created new suits of clothes out of nothing at all, so that the Tailor grew rich and held his head up in the world.

As time went along he laid heavier and heavier tasks upon the Demon's back and demanded of him more and more; but all the while the Demon kept his own counsel, and said never a word.

One morning, as the Tailor sat in his shop window taking the world easy—for he had little or nothing to do now—he heard a great hubbub in the street below, and when he looked down he saw that it was the King's daughter passing by. It was the first time that the Tailor had seen her, and when he saw her his heart stood still within him, and then began fluttering like a little bird, for one so beautiful was not to be met with in the four corners of the world. Then she was gone.

All that day the little Tailor could do nothing but sit and think of the princess, and the next morning when the Demon came he was thinking of her still.

"What hast thou for me to do today?" said the Demon, as he always said of a morning.

The little Tailor was waiting for the question.

"I would like you," said he, "to send to the King's palace and to ask him to let me have his daughter for my wife."

"Thou shalt have thy desire," said the Demon. Thereupon he smote his hands together like a clap of thunder, and instantly the walls of the room clove asunder, and there came out

• • •

four-and-twenty handsome youths, clad in cloth of gold and silver. After these four-and-twenty there came another one who was the chief of them all, and before whom, splendid as they were, the four-and-twenty paled like stars in daylight. "Go to the King's palace," said the Demon to that one, "and deliver this message: The Tailor of Tailors, the Master of Masters, and One Greater than a King asks for his daughter to wife."

"To hear is to obey," said the other, and bowed his forehead to the earth.

Never was there such a hubbub in the town as when those five-and-twenty, in their clothes of silver and gold, rode through the streets to the King's palace. As they came near, the gates of the palace flew open before them, and the King himself came out to meet them. The leader of the five-and-twenty leaped from his horse and, kissing the ground before the King, delivered his message: "The Tailor of Tailors, the Master of Masters, and One Greater than a King asks for thy daughter to wife."

When the King heard what the messenger said, he thought and pondered a long time.

◆◆◆

At last he said, "If he who sent you is the Master of Masters, and greater than a King, let him send me an asking gift such as no King could send."

"It shall be as you desire," said the messenger, and thereupon the five-and-twenty rode away as they had come, followed by crowds of people.

The next morning when the Demon came the Tailor was ready and waiting for him. "What hast thou for me to do today?" said the evil one.

• • •

"I want," said the tailor, "a gift to send to the King such as no other King could send him."

"Thou shalt have thy desire," said the Demon. Thereupon he smote his hands together and summoned not only the five-and-twenty young men, but fifty more youths, all clad in clothes more splendid than the others.

All of the fifty sat upon coal-black horses, with saddles of silver and housings of silk and velvet embroidered with gold. In the midst of all the five-and-seventy there rode a youth in cloth of silver embroidered in pearls. In his hand he bore something wrapped in a white napkin, and that was the present for the King such as no other King could give. So said the Demon: "Take it to the royal palace and tell his majesty that it is from the Tailor of Tailors, the Master of Masters, and One Greater than a King."

"To hear is to obey," said the young man, and then they all rode away.

When they came to the palace the gates flew open before them, and the King came out to meet them. The young man who bore the present dismounted and prostrated himself in the dust, and, when the King bade him arise,

he unwrapped the napkin and gave to the King a goblet made of one single ruby, and filled to the brim with pieces of gold. Moreover, the cup was of such a kind that whenever it was emptied of its money it instantly became full again. "The Tailor of Tailors, the Master of Masters, and One Greater than a King sends Your Majesty this goblet and bids me, his ambassador, to ask for your daughter," said the young man.

When the King saw what had been sent him he was filled with amazement. "Surely," said he to himself, "there can be no end to the power of one who can give such a gift as this." Then to the messenger, "Tell your master that he shall have my daughter for his wife if he will build

•••

over yonder a palace such as no man ever saw or no King ever lived in before."

"It shall be done," said the young man, and then they all went away, as the others had done the day before.

The next morning when the Demon appeared the Tailor was ready for him. "Build me," said he, "such and such a palace in such and such a place."

And the Demon said, "It shall be done." He smote his hands together, and instantly there came a cloud of mist that covered and hid the spot where the palace was to be built. Out from the cloud there came such a banging and hammering and clapping and clattering as the people of that town never heard before. Then when evening had come the cloud arose, and there, where the King had pointed out, stood a splendid palace as white as snow, with roofs and domes of gold and silver. As the King stood looking and wondering at this sight, there came five hundred young men riding, and one in the midst of all who wore a golden crown on his head, and upon his body a long robe stiff with diamonds and pearls. "We come," said he,

• • •

"from the Tailor of Tailors, the Master of Masters, and One Greater than a King, to ask you to let him have your daughter for his wife."

"Tell him to come," cried the King in admiration, "for the princess is his!"

The next morning when the Demon came he found the Tailor dancing and shouting for joy. "The princess is mine!" he cried, "So make me ready for her."

"It shall be done," said the Demon, and thereupon he began to make the Tailor ready for his wedding. He brought him to a marble bath of water, in which he washed away all that was coarse and ugly, and from which the little man came forth as beautiful as the sun. Then the Demon clad him in the finest linen and covered him with clothes such as even the Emperor of India never wore. Then he smote his hands together, and the wall of the tailor shop opened as it had done twice before, and there came forth forty slaves clad in crimson and bearing bowls full of money in their hands. After them came two leading a horse as white as snow, with a saddle of gold studded with diamonds and rubies and emeralds and sapphires. After came a bodyguard of twenty warriors clad in gold armor. Then the Tailor mounted his horse and rode away to the King's palace, and as he rode the slaves scattered the money amongst the crowd, who scrambled for it and cheered the Tailor to the skies.

That night the princess and the Tailor were married, and all the town was lit with bonfires and fireworks. The two rode away in the

•••

midst of a great crowd of nobles and courtiers to the palace which the Demon had built for the Tailor; and, as the princess gazed upon him, she thought that she had never beheld so noble and handsome a man as her husband. So she and the Tailor were the happiest couple in the world.

But the next morning the Demon appeared as he had appeared ever since the Tailor had let him out of the bottle, only now he grinned till his teeth shone and his face turned black. "What hast thou for me to do?" said he, and at the words the Tailor's heart began to quake, for he remembered what was to happen to him when he could find the Demon no more work to do—that his neck was to be wrung—and now he began to see that he had all that he could ask for in the world. Yes; what was there to ask for now?

"I have nothing more for you to do," said he to the Demon; "you have done all that man could ask—you may go now."

"Go!" cried the Demon. "I shall not go until I have done all that I have to do. Give me work, or I shall wring your neck." And his fingers began to twitch.

•••

Then the Tailor began to see into what a net he had fallen. He began to tremble like one in an ague. He turned his eyes up and down, for he did not know where to look for aid. Suddenly, as he looked out of the window, a thought struck him. “Maybe,” thought he, “I can give the Demon such a task that even he cannot do it.” “Yes, yes!” he cried. “I have thought of something for you to do. Make me out yonder in front of my palace a lake of water a mile long and a mile wide, and let it be lined throughout with white marble, and filled with water as clear as crystal.”

•••

"It shall be done," said the Demon. As he spoke he spat in the air, and instantly a thick fog arose from the earth and hid everything from sight. Then presently from the midst of the fog there came a great noise of chipping and hammering, of digging and delving, of rushing and gurgling. All day the noise and the fog continued, and then at sunset the one ceased and the other cleared away. The poor Tailor looked out the window, and when he saw what he saw his teeth chattered in his head, for there was a lake a mile long and a mile broad, lined within with white marble, and filled with water as clear as crystal, and he knew that the Demon would come the next morning for another task to do.

That night he slept little or none, and when the seventh hour of the morning came the castle began to rock and tremble, and there stood the Demon, and his hair bristled and his eyes shone like sparks of fire. "What hast thou for me to do?" said he, and the poor Tailor could do nothing but look at him with a face as white as dough.

"What hast thou for me to do?" said the Demon again, and then at last the Tailor found his wits and his tongue from sheer terror. "Look," said he, "at the great mountain over yonder; remove it, and make in its place a level plain with fields and orchards and gardens." And he thought to himself when he had spoken, "Surely, even the Demon cannot do that."

"It shall be done," said the Demon, and, so saying, he stamped his heel upon the ground. Instantly the earth began to tremble and quake, and there came a great rumbling like the sound of thunder. A cloud of darkness gathered in the sky, until at last all was as black as the blackest midnight. Then came a roaring and a cracking and a crashing, such as man never heard before. All day it continued, until the time of the setting of the sun, when suddenly the uproar ceased, and the darkness cleared away; and when the Tailor looked out of the window the mountain was gone, and in its place were fields and orchards and gardens.

It was very beautiful to see, but when the Tailor beheld it his knees began to smite together, and the sweat ran down his face in streams. All that night he walked up and down and up and down, but he could not think of one other task for the Demon to do.

• • •

When the next morning came the Demon appeared like a whirlwind. His face was black as ink and smoke, and sparks of fire flew from his nostrils.

"What have you for me to do?" cried he.

"I have nothing for you to do!" piped the poor Tailor.

"Nothing?" cried the Demon.

"Nothing."

"Then prepare to die."

"Stop!" said the Tailor, falling on his knees. "Let me first see my wife."

•••

"So be it," said the Demon, and if he had been wiser he would have said "No."

When the Tailor came to the princess, he flung himself on his face and began to weep and wail. The princess asked him what was the matter, and at last, by dint of question, got the story from him, piece by piece. When she had it all she began laughing. "Why did you not come to me before," said she, "instead of making all this trouble and uproar for nothing at all? I will give the Monster a task to do." She plucked a single curling hair from her head. "Here," said she, "let him take this hair and make it straight."

The Tailor was full of doubt; nevertheless, as there was nothing better to do, he took it to the Demon.

"Hast thou found me a task to do?" cried the Demon.

"Yes," said the Tailor. "It is only a little thing. Here is a hair from my wife's head; take it and make it straight."

When the Demon heard what was the task that the Tailor had set him to do he laughed aloud; but that was because he did not know. He took the hair and stroked it between his

•••

thumb and finger, and, when he had done, it curled more than ever. Then he looked serious, and slapped it between his palms, and that did not better matters, for it curled as much as ever. Then he frowned, and began beating the hair with his palm upon his knees, and that only made it worse. All that day he labored and strove at his task trying to make that one little hair straight, and, when the sun set, there was the hair just as crooked as ever.

•••

Then, as the great round sun sank red behind the trees, the Demon knew that he was beaten. "I am conquered! I am conquered!" he howled, and flew away, bellowing so dreadfully that all the world trembled.

So ends the story, with only this to say:

Where man's strength fails,
woman's wit prevails.

For, to my mind, the princess—not to speak of her husband the little Tailor—did more with a single little hair and her mother wit than King Solomon with all his wisdom.

"Is it possible that someone is trickier than I?"

The Man Whose Trade Was Tricks

Georgian folktale as told by George and Helen Papashvily

There was, there was, and yet there was not, there was once a king who, like all kings, wanted to believe he was the trickiest man in the whole world.

During the day when his court stood near to applaud each word he spoke, he felt sure of this. But at night when sleep was slow he worried.

Is it possible, is it really possible, he would think to himself, that there might be someone who is trickier than I?

Finally he could endure it no longer, and he called his viziers together.

• • •

"Go," he commanded them, "and find the trickiest man in my kingdom and bring him here before me. I will match myself against him. If he loses he must be my slave for life."

The viziers set out and in their travels they met many clever men—such clever men, in fact, that they refused to go back and match themselves against the king for no better reward than a promise they might be slaves.

The viziers grew desperate.

At last one night they came through a fertile valley bordered with thick forests into the street of a poor village. Now this village, you should know, was not poor because it was a lazy village or a stupid village. It was poor because the king owned the valley and all the forest beyond. Each year he took such a heavy rent that no matter how hard the villagers worked when harvest time came, nothing was left for them but the middlings of their own wheat and a few crooked tree stumps.

But poor as this village was, they knew how to act like rich men. They called the viziers to the best supper they could cook and afterward, for their entertainment, built a campfire and told stories.

* * *

As the evening sharpened itself to a point, the viziers noticed that one man, Shahkro, was better than all the rest at guessing riddles, and remembering poems, and describing his adventures.

"Let us see if he will go with us and match himself against the king," whispered the viziers to each other.

At first when they asked Shahkro he refused, but finally after some persuasion he said, "I will go with you, but I will go just like this. Without my hat and without my cherkasska."

•••

And exactly that way they brought him before the king.

"Sit down," the king said. "So you think you are the trickiest man in my kingdom?"

"Tricking is my trade," Shahkro answered.

"Try to trick me then," the king commanded. "But I warn you," he added, "it cannot be done for I am so tricky myself."

"I can see that," Shahkro said. "I wish I had known all this before. I would have come prepared. As it was

•••

I left in such a hurry I didn't stop for my hat or my cherkasska, to say nothing of my tools."

"What tools?"

"Why, the tools I use for tricking people."

"Go and get them."

"That's not so easy. Naturally, as I'm sure you know from your own experience, I can't just bundle them together as though they were something ordinary. I need wagons."

"Wagons?" said the king. "How many wagons?"

"About a hundred with a hundred horses to pull them."

"Take them from my stable but come right back."

"Certainly," Shahkro said. "With luck I should have everything loaded in five or six months."

"Five or six months?"

• • •

"I'll need to bring *all* my tools if I must trick you."

"Well, come back as soon as you can."

"By the way," Shahkro said when the wagons were brought and he was ready to drive off, "if I can't trick you I know I must be your slave for the rest of my life, but just suppose I win, what then?"

"But you can't win," the king told him.

"I know I can't, but suppose I did."

"Well, what do you want?"

"Something you wouldn't miss if you gave it to me."

"I agree," said the king.

Shahkro went home at a fast trot, called all the villagers together,

•••

gave them each a horse and wagon, and working side by side they sowed and harvested a crop large enough to last them for ten years.

"At least we have this much out of it," Shahkro said, when the last load of grain came creaking into the barn. "Now bring me all the empty wineskins you can find."

When these were collected, Shahkro blew them full of air and piled them on the wagons and rode back to the palace.

The king was waiting impatiently for him in the great hall surrounded by all his nobles dressed in their richest costumes.

"Let us begin," the king said.

"I must unpack my tools," Shahkro told him.

"I will send servants to do that," the king said.

While they were waiting the king's dog ran into the room and, noticing a stranger was there, he came over and sniffed Shahkro's legs to make his acquaintance.

• • •

Shahkro bent his head and blew very lightly in the dog's ear. The dog, of course, in turn licked Shahkro's ear.

"This is awful news!" Shahkro jumped up from his chair. "Awful! Where's my hat? Where's my coat? I beg you loan me the fastest horse in your own stable. My dear wife whom I left well and happy yesterday, is dying."

"How do you know?" cried the king.

"How does he know?" cried the court.

"Your dog, as you saw, whispered it in my ear just now."

Everyone was sorry and the king ordered the best horse in his stable saddled, a full-blooded black Arabian, and Shahkro rode away home.

He stayed there long enough to sell the horse for a good price and buy a black donkey. Then he put the horse's saddle and bridle on the donkey and went back to town.

•••

The king was waiting in the courtyard and when he saw Shahkro jogging along he cried out, "Where is my horse?"

"Horse?" Shahkro said. "Horse! Oh King, have your joke at my expense. I am only a poor man. But I never thought you would do a thing like this to me. Send me home to my sick wife on a horse that changes himself back and forth to a donkey as it suits his pleasure."

"That's impossible," the king said. "I've had that horse for five years."

"Impossible or not," Shahkro answered. "Here I am the same as I started out for home five days ago. Here is the same bridle in my hands. Here is the same black animal under me. And it's a donkey."

The king looked at the saddle and at the bridle. He ran his hand over the donkey's flank. "Well, all I can say in apology is that he never did it while I rode him. But let's forget all that. When are you going to try to trick me?"

"Right now," Shahkro said. "Sit down. Answer me a question. You claimed you were a trickster. Did you ever use any tools?"

"No."

•••

"Then why did you think I would? So there I tricked you once. In all the years you had your dog, did he ever talk to you?"

"No."

"Then why did you think he would talk to me? I tricked you twice. In all the years you had your black horse did he ever turn into a donkey for you?"

"No."

"Then why should he for me? There I tricked you three times. Now pay me and I will go."

The king saw he had one last chance to redeem his reputation as a trickster so he said, "Remember, for your reward I promised only what I wouldn't miss. You must choose something I never use or otherwise I would miss it. Now what shall it be?"

"Your head," Shahkro answered.

When the king heard this he began to shake and turn so green that Shahkro took pity on him. "Wait," he said, "I will take another reward. Because on second thought you do use your head. It keeps your hat from lying on your shoulders. Give me instead your forest and all the fields around it for my village people to use for their own."

•••

"Certainly," said the king, and he called his viziers and sealed the agreement right there and gave it to Shahkro. "And now I don't want to keep you for I know you are anxious to get home."

Shahkro went back to his village and in honor he lived there all his life.

As for the king, after that he didn't have to worry anymore whether or not he was the trickiest man in the world, so I suppose he slept very well. Or maybe because he was a king he found a new worry to keep him awake.

HOW THE TORTOISE BECAME

Ted Hughes

Long ago when the world was brand new, before animals or birds, the sun rose into the sky and brought the first day.

The flowers jumped up and stared round astonished. Then from every side, from under leaves and from behind rocks, creatures began to appear.

In those days the colours were much better than they are now, much brighter. And the air sparkled because it had never been used.

But don't think everything was so easy.

• • •

To begin with, all the creatures were pretty much alike—very different from what they are now. They had no idea what they were going to become. Some wanted to become linnets, some wanted to become lions, some wanted to become other things. The ones that wanted to become lions practised at being lions—and by and by, sure enough, they began to turn into lions. So, the ones that wanted to become linnets practised at being linnets, and slowly they turned into linnets. And so on.

But there were other creatures that came about in other ways. . . .

When God made a creature, he first of all shaped it in clay. Then he baked it in the ovens of the sun until it was hard. Then he took it out of the oven and, when it was cool, breathed life into it. Last of all, he pulled its skin onto it like a tight jersey.

All the animals got different skins. If it was a cold day, God would give to the animals he made on that day a dense, woolly skin. Snow was falling heavily when he made the sheep and the bears.

•••

If it was a hot day, the new animals got a thin skin. On the day he made greyhounds and dachshunds and boys and girls, the weather was so hot God had to wear a sun hat and was calling endlessly for iced drinks.

Now on the day he made Torto, God was so hot the sweat was running down onto the tips of his fingers.

After baking Torto in the oven, God took him out to cool. Then he flopped back in his chair and ordered Elephant to fan him with its ears. He had made Elephant only a few days before and was very pleased with its big flapping ears. At last he thought that Torto must surely be cool.

"He's had as long as I usually give a little thing like him," he said, and picking up Torto, he breathed life into him. As he did so, he found out his mistake.

Torto was not cool. Far from it. On that hot day, with no cooling breezes, Torto had remained scorching hot. Just as he was when he came out of the oven.

"Ow!" roared God. He dropped Torto and went hopping away on one leg to the other end of his workshop, shaking his burnt fingers.

•••

"Ow, ow, ow!" he roared again, and plunged his hand into a dish of butter to cure the burns.

Torto meanwhile lay on the floor, just alive, groaning with the heat.

"Oh, I'm so hot!" he moaned. "So hot! The heat. Oh, the heat!"

God was alarmed that he had given Torto life before he was properly cooled.

"Just a minute, Torto," he said, "I'll have a nice, thin, cooling skin on you in a jiffy. Then you'll feel better."

•••

But Torto wanted no skin. He was too hot as it was.

"No, no!" he cried. "I shall stifle. Let me go without a skin for a few days. Let me cool off first."

"That's impossible," said God. "All creatures must have skins."

"No, no!" cried Torto, wiping the sweat from his little brow. "No skin!"

"Yes!" cried God.

"No!" cried Torto.

"Yes!"

"No!"

God made a grab at Torto, who ducked and ran like lightning under a cupboard. Without any skin to cumber his movements, Torto felt very light and agile.

"Come out!" roared God, and got down on his knees to grope under the cupboard for Torto.

In a flash, Torto was out from under the other end of the cupboard, and while God was still struggling to his feet, he ran out through the door and into the world, without a skin.

The first thing he did was to go to a cool pond and plunge straight into it. There he lay, for several days, just cooling off. Then he came out and began to live among the other creatures. But he was still very hot. Whenever he felt his own heat getting too much for him, he retired to his pond to cool off in the water. In this way, he found life pleasant enough.

Except for one thing. The other creatures didn't approve of Torto.

They all had skins. When they saw Torto without a skin, they were horrified.

"But he has no skin!" cried Porcupine.

"It's disgusting!" cried Yak. "It's indecent!"

• • •

"He's not normal. Leave him to himself," said Sloth.

So all the animals began to ignore Torto. But they couldn't ignore him completely, because he was a wonderfully swift runner, and whenever they held a race, he won it. He was so nimble without a skin that none of the other creatures could hope to keep up with him.

"I'm a genius runner," he said. "You should respect me. I am faster than the lot of you put together. I was made different."

But the animals still ignored him. Even when they had to give him the prizes for winning all the races, they still ignored him.

"Torto is a very swift mover," they said. "And perhaps swifter than any of us. But what sort of a creature is he? No skin!"

And they all turned up their noses.

At first, Torto didn't care at all. When the animals collected together, with all their fur brushed and combed and set neatly, he strolled among them, smiling happily, naked.

"When will this disgusting creature learn to behave?" cried Turkey, loudly enough for everyone to hear.

•••

"Just take no notice of him," said Alligator, and lumbered round, in his heavy armour, to face in the opposite direction.

All the animals turned round to face in the opposite direction.

When Torto went up to Grizzly Bear to ask what everyone was looking at, Grizzly Bear pretended to have a fly in his ear. When he went to Armadillo, Armadillo gathered up all his sons and daughters and led them off without a word or a look.

"So that's your game, is it?" said Torto to himself. Then aloud, he said: "Never mind. Wait till it comes to the races."

When the races came, later in the afternoon, Torto won them all. But nobody cheered. He collected the prizes and went off to his pond alone.

"They're jealous of me," he said. "That's why they ignore me.

•••

But I'll punish them: I'll go on winning all the races."

That night, God came to Torto and begged him to take a proper skin before it was too late. Torto shook his head:

"The other animals are snobs," he said. "Just because they are covered with a skin, they think everyone else should be covered with one too. That's snobbery. But I shall teach them not to be snobs by making them respect me. I shall go on winning all the races."

And so he did. But still the animals didn't respect him. In fact, they grew to dislike him more and more.

One day there was a very important race meeting, and all the animals collected at the usual place. But the minute Torto arrived they simply walked away. Simply got up and walked away. Torto sat on the racetrack and stared after them. He felt really left out.

"Perhaps," he thought sadly, "it would be better if I had a skin. I mightn't be able to run then, but at least I would have friends. I have no friends. Besides, after all this practice, I would still be able to run quite fast."

•••

But as soon as he said that he felt angry with himself.

"No!" he cried. "They are snobs. I shall go on winning their races in spite of them. I shall teach them a lesson."

And he got up from where he was sitting and followed them. He found them all in one place, under a tree. And the races were being run.

"Hey!" he called as he came up to them. "What about me?"

But at that moment, Tiger held up a sign in front of him. On the sign, Torto read: "Creatures without skins are not allowed to enter."

Torto went home and brooded. God came up to him.

"Well, Torto," said God kindly, "would you like a skin yet?"

Torto thought deeply.

"Yes," he said at last, "I would like a skin. But only a very special sort of skin."

"And what sort of a skin is that?" asked God.

"I would like," said Torto, "a skin that I can put on, or take off, just whenever I please."

God frowned.

"I'm afraid," he said, "I have none like that."

• • •

"Then make one," replied Torto. "You're God."

God went away and came back within an hour.

"Do you want a beautiful skin?" he asked. "Or do you mind if it's very ugly?"

"I don't care what sort of a skin it is," said Torto, "so long as I can take it off and put it back on again just whenever I please."

God went away again, and again came back within an hour.

"Here it is. That's the best I can do."

"What's this!" cried Torto. "But it's horrible!"

"Take it or leave it," said God, and walked away.

•••

Torto examined the skin. It was tough, rough, and stiff.

"It's like a coconut," he said. "With holes in it."

And so it was. Only it was shiny. When he tried it on, he found it quite snug. It had only one disadvantage. He could move only very slowly in it.

"What's the hurry?" he said to himself then. "When it comes to moving, who can move faster than me?"

And he laughed. Suddenly he felt delighted. Away he went to where the animals were still running their races.

As he came near to them, he began to think that perhaps his skin was a little rough and ready. But he checked himself:

"Why should I dress up for them?" he said. "This rough old thing will do. The races are the important thing."

Tiger lowered his notice and stared in dismay as Torto swaggered past him. All the animals were now turning and staring, nudging each other, and turning, and staring.

"That's a change, anyway," thought Torto.

Then, as usual, he entered for all the races.

•••

The animals began to talk and laugh among themselves as they pictured Torto trying to run in his heavy new clumsy skin.

"He'll look silly, and then how we'll laugh." And they all laughed.

But when he took his skin off at the starting post, their laughs turned to frowns.

He won all the races, then climbed back into his skin to collect the prizes. He strutted in front of all the animals.

"Now it's my turn to be snobbish," he said to himself.

Then he went home, took off his skin, and slept sweetly. Life was perfect for him.

This went on for many years. But though the animals would now speak to him, they remembered what he had been. That didn't worry Torto, however. He became very fond of his skin. He began to keep it on at night when he came home after the races. He began to do everything in it, except actually race. He crept around slowly, smiling at the leaves, letting the days pass.

There came a time when there were no races for several weeks. During all this time Torto

never took his skin off once. Until, when the first race came round at last, he found he could not take his skin off at all, no matter how he pushed and pulled. He was stuck inside it. He strained and squeezed and gasped, but it was no use. He was stuck.

However, he had already entered for all the races, so he had to run.

He lined up, in his skin, at the start, alongside Hare, Greyhound, Cheetah, and Ostrich. They were all great runners, but usually he could beat the lot of them easily. The crowd stood agog.

"Perhaps," Torto was thinking, "my skin won't make much difference. I've never really tried to run my very fastest in it."

• • •

The starter's pistol cracked, and away went Greyhound, Hare, Cheetah, and Ostrich, neck and neck. Where was Torto?

The crowd roared with laughter.

Torto had fallen on his face and had not moved an inch. At his first step, cumbered by his stiff, heavy skin, he had fallen on his face. But he tried. He climbed back onto his feet and made one stride, slowly, then a second stride, and was just about to make a third when the race was over and Cheetah had won. Torto had moved not quite three paces. How the crowd laughed!

And so it was with all the races. In no one race did Torto manage to make more than three steps before it was over.

The crowd was enjoying itself. Torto was weeping with shame.

After the last race, he turned to crawl home. He only wanted to hide. But though the other animals had let him go off alone when he had the prizes, now they came alongside him, in a laughing, mocking crowd.

"Who's the slowest of all the creatures?" they shouted.

◆◆◆

"Torto is!"

"Who's the slowest of all the creatures?"

"Torto is!" all the way home.

After that, Torto tried to keep himself out of sight, but the other animals never let him rest. Whenever any of them chanced to see him, they would shout at the tops of their voices:

"Who's the slowest of all the creatures?"

And every other creature within hearing would answer, at the tops of their voices:

"Torto is!"

And that is how Torto came to be known as "Tortoise."

TOM-TIT-TOT

English folktale as told by
Flora Annie Steel

Once upon a time there was a woman and she baked five pies. But when they came out of the oven they were overbaked, and the crust was far too hard to eat. So she said to her daughter:

"Daughter," says she, "put them pies onto the shelf and leave 'em there awhile. Surely they'll come again in time."

By that, you know, she meant that they would become softer. But her daughter said to herself, "If Mother says the pies will come again, why shouldn't I eat these now?"

•••

So, having good young teeth, she set to work and ate the lot, first and last.

Now when supper time came the woman said to her daughter, "Go you and get one of the pies. They are sure to have come again by now."

Then the girl went and looked, but of course there was nothing but the empty dishes.

So back she came and said, "No, Mother, they ain't come again."

"Not one o' them?" asked the mother, taken aback like.

"Not one o' them," says the daughter, quite confident.

"Well," says the mother, "come again, or not come again, I will have one of them pies for my supper."

"But you can't," says the daughter. "How can you if they ain't come? And they ain't, as sure's sure."

"But I can," says the mother, getting angry. "Go you at once, child, and bring me the best of them. My teeth must just tackle it."

"Best or worst is all one," answered the daughter, quite sulky, "for I've ate the lot, so you can't have one till it comes again—so there!"

•••

Well, the mother she bounced up to see, but half an eye told her there was nothing save the empty dishes, so she was dished up herself and done for.

So, having no supper, she sat her down on the doorstep and, bringing out her distaff, began to spin. And as she spun she sang:

> My daughter ha' ate five pies today,
> My daughter ha' ate five pies today,
> My daughter ha' ate five pies today,

for you see, she was quite flabbergasted and fair astonished.

Now the King of that country happened to be coming down the street, and he heard the song going on and on, but could not quite make out the words. So he stopped his horse and asked:

"What is that you are singing, my good woman?"

Now the mother, though horrified at her daughter's

appetite, did not want other folk, leastwise the King, to know about it, so she sang instead:

My daughter ha' spun five skeins today,
My daughter ha' spun five skeins today,
My daughter ha' spun five skeins today.

"Five skeins!" cried the King. "By my garter and my crown, I never heard tell of anyone who could do that! Look you here, I have been searching for a wife, and your daughter who can spin five skeins a day is the very one for me. Only mind you, though for eleven months of the year she shall be Queen indeed, and have all she likes to eat, all the gowns she likes to get, all the company she likes to keep, and everything her heart desires, in the twelfth month she must set to work and spin five skeins a day, and if she does not she must die. Come! is it a bargain?"

So the mother agreed. She thought what a grand marriage it was for her daughter. And as for the five skeins? Time enough to bother about them when the year came round. There was many a slip between cup and lip, and likely as not, the King would have forgotten all about it by then.

•••

Anyhow, her daughter would be Queen for eleven months. So they were married, and for eleven months the bride was happy as happy could be. She had everything she liked to eat, and all the gowns she liked to get, all the company she cared to keep, and everything her heart desired. And her husband the King was kind as kind could be. But in the tenth month she began to think of those five skeins and wonder if the King remembered. And in the eleventh month she began to dream about them as well. But never a word did the King, her husband, say about them, so she hoped he had forgotten.

But on the very last day of the eleventh month, the King, her husband, led her into a room she had never set eyes on before. It had one window, and there was nothing in it but a stool and a spinning wheel.

•••

"Now, my dear," he said quite kind-like, "you will be shut in here tomorrow morning with some food and some flax, and if by evening you have not spun five skeins, your head will come off."

Well, she was fair frightened, for she had always been such a senseless, thoughtless girl that she had never learned to spin at all. So what she was to do on the morrow she could not tell. For you see she had no one to help her, for of course now that she was Queen her mother didn't live nigh her. So she just locked the door of her room, sat down on a stool, and cried and cried and cried until her eyes were all red.

Now as she sat sobbing and crying she heard a queer little noise at the bottom of the door. At first she thought it was a mouse. Then she thought it must be something knocking.

So she upped and opened the door and what did she see? Why! a small, little, black Thing with a long tail that whisked round and round ever so fast.

"What are you crying for?" said that Thing, making a bow and twirling its tail so fast that she could scarcely see it.

"What's that to you?" said she, shrinking a bit, for that Thing was very queer-like.

"Don't look at my tail if you're frightened," says That, smirking. "Look at my toes. Ain't they beautiful?"

And sure enough, That had on buckled shoes with high heels and big bows, ever so smart.

So she kind of forgot about the tail, and wasn't so frightened, and when That asked her again

•••

why she was crying, she upped and said, "It won't do no good if I do."

"You don't know that," says That, twirling its tail faster and faster, and sticking out its toes. "Come, tell me, there's a good girl."

"Well," says she, "it can't do any harm if it doesn't do good." So she dried her pretty eyes and told That all about the pies, and the skeins, and everything from first to last.

And then that little, black Thing nearly burst with laughing. "If that is all, it's easy mended!" it says. "I'll come to your window every morning, take the flax, and bring it back spun into five skeins at night. Come! shall it be a bargain?"

Now she, for all she was so senseless and thoughtless, said, cautious-like:

"But what is your pay?"

Then That twirled its tail so fast you couldn't see it,

and stuck out its beautiful toes, and smirked and looked out of the corners of its eyes. "I will give you three guesses every night to guess my name, and if you haven't guessed it before the month is up, why"—and That twirled its tail faster and stuck out its toes further, and smirked and sniggered more than ever—"you shall be mine, my beauty."

Three guesses every night for a whole month! She felt sure she would be able for so much. And there was no other way out of the business, so she just said, "Yes! I agree!"

And oh! how That twirled its tail, and bowed, and smirked, and stuck out its beautiful toes.

Well, the very next day her husband led her to the strange room again, and there was the day's food, and a spinning wheel and a great bundle of flax.

•••

"There you are, my dear," says he as polite as polite. "And remember! if there are not five whole skeins tonight, I fear your head will come off!"

At that she began to tremble, and after he had gone away and locked the door, she was just thinking of a good cry when she heard a queer knocking at the window. She upped at once and opened it, and sure enough there was the small, little, black Thing sitting on the window ledge, dangling its beautiful toes and twirling its tail so that you could scarcely see it.

"Good morning, my beauty," says That. "Come! hand over the flax, sharp, there's a good girl."

So she gave That the flax and shut the window and, you may be sure, ate her food, for as you know she had a good appetite and the King, her husband, had promised to give her everything she liked to eat. So she ate to her heart's content, and when evening came and she heard that queer knocking at the window again, she upped and opened it, and there was the small, little, black Thing with five spun skeins on his arm!

•••

And it twirled its tail faster than ever, and stuck out its beautiful toes, and bowed and smirked and gave her the five skeins.

Then That said, "And now, my beauty, what is That's name?"

And she answered quite easy-like:

"That is Bill."

"No, it ain't," says That, and twirled its tail.

"Then That is Ned," says she.

"No, it ain't," says That, and twirled its tail faster.

"Well," says she a bit more thoughtful, "That is Mark."

"No, it ain't," says That, and laughs and laughs and laughs, and twirls its tail so as you couldn't see it, as away it flew.

Well, when the King, her husband, came in, he was fine and pleased to see the five skeins all ready for him, for he was fond of his pretty wife.

"I shall not have to order your head off, my dear," says he. "And I hope all the other days will pass as happily." Then he said good night and locked the door and left her.

But next morning they brought her fresh flax and even more delicious foods. And the small,

•••

little, black Thing came knocking at the window, and stuck out its beautiful toes and twirled its tail faster and faster, and took away the bundle of flax and brought it back all spun into five skeins by evening. Then That made her guess three times what That's name was, but she could not guess right, and That laughed and laughed and laughed as it flew away.

Now every morning and evening the same thing happened, and every evening she had her three guesses, but she never guessed right.

And every day the small, little, black Thing laughed louder and louder and smirked more and more, and looked at her quite maliceful out of the corners of its eyes until she began to get frightened, and instead of eating all the fine foods left for her, spent the day in trying to think of names to say. But she never hit upon the right one.

• • •

So it came to the last day of the month but one, and when the small, little, black Thing arrived in the evening with the five skeins of flax all ready spun, it could hardly say for smirking:

"Ain't you got That's name yet?"

So says she—for she had been reading her Bible:

"Is That Nicodemus?"

"No, it ain't," says That, and twirled its tail faster than you could see.

"Is That Samuel?" says she, all of a flutter.

"No, it ain't, my beauty," chuckles That, looking maliceful.

"Well—is That Methuselah?" says she, inclined to cry.

Then That just fixes her with eyes like a coal afire and says, "No, it ain't that neither, so there is only tomorrow night and then you'll be mine, my beauty."

And away the small, little, black Thing flew, its tail twirling and whisking so fast that you couldn't see it.

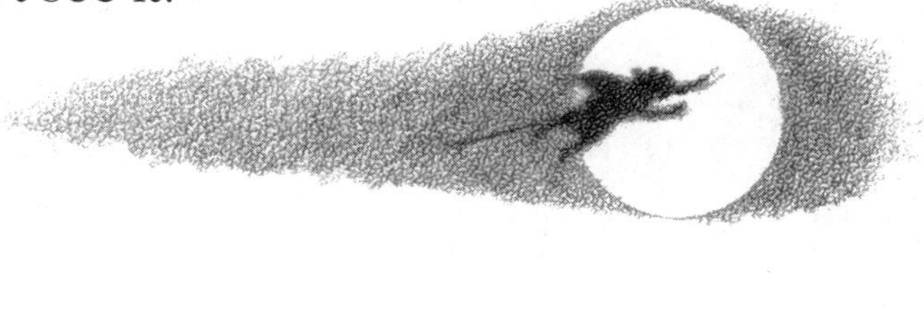

Well she felt so bad she couldn't even cry, but she heard the King, her husband, coming to the door, so she made bold to be cheerful and tried to smile when he said, "Well done, wife! Five skeins again! I shall not have to order your head off after all, my dear, of that I'm quite sure, so let us enjoy ourselves." Then he bade the servants bring supper, and a stool for him to sit beside his Queen, and down they sat, lover-like, side by side.

But the poor Queen could eat nothing. She could not forget the small, little, black Thing. And the King hadn't eaten but a mouthful or two when he began to laugh, and he laughed so long and so loud that at last the poor Queen, all lackadaisical as she was, said:

"Why do you laugh so?"

•••

"At something I saw today, my love," says the King. "I was out a-hunting, and by chance I came to a place I'd never been in before. It was in a wood, and there was an old chalk pit there, and out of the chalk pit there came a queer kind of a sort of a humming, bumming noise. So I got off my horse to see what made it, and went quite quiet to the edge of the pit and looked down. And what do you think I saw? The funniest, queerest, smallest, little black Thing you ever set eyes upon. And it had a little spinning wheel and it was spinning away for dear life, but the wheel didn't go so fast as its tail, and that spun round and round—ho-ho-ha-ha! —you never saw the like. And its little feet had buckled shoes and bows on them, and they went up and down in a desperate hurry. And all the time that small,

•••

little, black Thing kept humming and booming away at these words:

> Name me, name me not,
> Who'll guess it's Tom-Tit-Tot.

Well, when she heard these words the Queen nearly jumped out of her skin for joy. She managed to say nothing, but ate her supper quite comfortably.

And she said no word when next morning the small, little, black Thing came for the flax, though it looked so gleeful and maliceful that she could hardly help laughing, knowing she had got the better of it. And when night came and she heard That knocking against the windowpanes, she put on a wry face and opened the window slowly as if she was afraid. But that Thing was as bold as brass and came right inside, grinning from ear to ear. And oh, my goodness! how That's tail was twirling and whisking!

"Well, my beauty," says That, giving her the five skeins all ready spun, "what's my name?"

Then she put down her lip and says, tearful-like, "Is—is—That—Solomon?"

•••

"No, it ain't," laughs That, smirking out of the corner of That's eye. And the small, little, black Thing came further into the room.

So she tried again—and this time she seemed hardly able to speak for fright.

"Well—is That—Zebedee?" she says.

"No, it ain't," cried the imp, full of glee. And it came quite close and stretched out its little black hands to her, and Oh-Oh-ITS TAIL . . . ! ! !

"Take time, my beauty," says That, sort of jeering-like, and its small, little, black eyes seemed to eat her up. "Take time! Remember! next guess and you're mine!"

Well, she backed just a wee bit from it, for it was just horrible to look at. But then she laughed

•••

out and pointed her finger at it and said, says she:

> Name me, name me not,
> *Your* name is
> *Tom*
> TIT
> *TOT.*

And you never heard such a shriek as that small, little, black Thing gave out. Its tail dropped down straight, its feet all crumpled up, and away That flew into the dark, and she never saw it no more.

And she lived happy ever after with her husband, the King.

The Snowman

Hans Christian Andersen

It crackles and creaks inside of me. It is so cold that it is a pleasure," said the snowman. "When the wind bites you, then you know you're alive. Look how the burning one gapes and stares." By "the burning one" he meant the sun, which was just about to set. "But she can't make me blink; I'll stare right back at her."

The snowman had two triangular pieces of tile for eyes, and a children's rake for a mouth, which meant that he had teeth. His birth had been greeted by the boys with shouts of joy,

•••

to the sound of sleigh bells and the cracking of whips.

The sun set and the moon rose, full and round, beautiful in the blue evening sky.

"There she is again, just in another place. She couldn't stay away." The snowman thought that the sun had returned. "I guess that I have cooled her off. But now she's welcome to stay up there, for it is pleasant with a bit of light, so that I can see. If only I knew how to move and get about, then I would go down to the lake and slide on the ice as the boys do. But I don't know how to run."

"Out! Out! Out!" barked the old watchdog, who was chained to his doghouse. He was hoarse and had been so ever since he had been refused entrance to the house. That was a long time ago now; but when the dog lived inside, it had lain next to the stove. "The sun will teach you to run. I saw what happened to last year's snowman and to the one the year before last. . . . Out! Out! Out! They are all gone."

"What do you mean by that, comrade?" asked the snowman. "How can that round one up there teach me to run?" By "that round one,"

•••

he meant the moon. "She ran when I looked straight into her eyes. Now she is trying to sneak back from another direction."

"You are ignorant," said the watchdog. "But you have only just been put together. The round one up there is called the moon. The other one is the sun and she will be back tomorrow. She will teach you how to run, right down to the lake. I've got a pain in my left hind leg and that means the weather is about to change."

"I don't understand him," thought the snowman, "but I have a feeling that he was saying something unpleasant. The hot one—the one that was here a moment ago and then went away, the one he called the sun—is no friend of mine. Not that she's done me any harm; it's just a feeling I have."

The weather did change. In the morning there was a heavy fog. During the day it lifted, the wind started to blow, and there was frost. The sun came out and what a beautiful sight it was! The hoarfrost made the forest appear like a coral reef; every tree and bush looked as if it were decked with white flowers. In the summer when they have leaves, you cannot see what intricate and lovely patterns the branches make. But now they looked like lace and were so brilliantly white that they seemed to radiate light. The weeping birch tree swayed in the wind as it did in summer. Oh, it was marvelous to see. As the sun rose higher in the sky its light grew sharper and its rays made everything appear as if it were covered with diamond dust. In the blanket of snow that lay upon the ground were large diamonds, blinking like a thousand small candles, whose light was whiter than snow.

"Isn't it unbelievably beautiful?" said a young girl who was taking a walk in the garden with a young man. "I think it's even lovelier now than it is in summer." And her eyes shone, as if the beauty of the garden were reflected in them.

They stopped near the snowman to admire the forest. "And a handsome fellow like that you won't see in the summer either," remarked the young man, pointing to the snowman.

The girl laughed and curtsied before the snowman, then she took the young man's hand in hers and the two of them danced across the snow, which crunched beneath their feet as if they were walking on grain.

"Who were they?" the snowman asked the dog. "You've been here on the farm longer than I have. Do you know them?"

"Certainly," answered the old dog. "She has patted me and he has given me bones. I would never bite either of them."

"Why do they walk hand in hand? I have never seen boys walk like that."

"They are engaged," the old dog sniffed. "Soon they will be moving into the same doghouse and will share each other's bones."

"Are they as important as you and I?" asked the snowman.

"They belong to the house and are our masters," replied the dog. "You certainly know precious little, even if you were only born yesterday. I wouldn't have believed such

• • •

ignorance existed if I hadn't heard it with my own ears. But I have both age and knowledge, and from them you acquire wisdom. I know everyone on the farm; and I have known better times, when I didn't have to stand here, chained up and frozen to the bone. . . . Out! Out! Get out!"

"I love to freeze," said the snowman. "Tell me about the time when you were young, but stop rattling your chain like that, it makes me shudder inside."

"Out! Out!" barked the old dog. "I was a puppy once. 'See that lovely little fellow,' they used to say, and I slept on a velvet chair. I lay in the lap of the master of the house and had my paws wiped with embroidered handkerchiefs. They kissed me and called me a sweetheart, and their little doggy-woggy. When I grew too big to lie in a lap they gave me to the housekeeper. She had a room

• • •

in the cellar.—You can look right into her window from where you are standing.—Down there I was the master. It wasn't as nicely furnished as upstairs, but it was much more comfortable. I had my own pillow to lie on, and the housekeeper gave me just as good food and more of it. Besides, upstairs there were children and they are a plague, always picking you up, squeezing you, and hugging you, and carrying you about as if you had no legs of your own to walk on. . . . Then there was the stove. In winter there is nothing as lovely as a stove. When it was really cold I used to crawl all the way under it. I still dream of being there, though it's a long time since I was there last. . . . Out! Out! Out!"

"Is a stove a thing of beauty?" asked the snowman. "Does it look like me?"

"You're as much alike as day and night. The stove's as black as coal; it has a long black neck with a brass collar around it. The fire's in the bottom.

•••

The stove lives on wood, which it eats so fast that it breathes fire out of its mouth. Ah! To lie near it or, better still, underneath it; until you have tried that you have no idea what comfort is. . . . You must be able to see it from where you are. That window, there, just look in."

And the snowman did and he saw the stove: a black, polished metal figure with brass fixtures. The little door at the bottom, through which ashes could be removed, had a window in it; and the snowman could see the light from the fire. A strange feeling of sadness and joy came over him. A feeling he had never experienced before. A feeling that all human beings know, except those who are made of snow.

"Why did you leave her?" The snowman somehow felt certain that the stove was of the female sex. "How could you bear to go away from such a lovely place?"

"I had to," answered the old watchdog. "They threw me out, put a chain around my neck, and here I am. And all I had done was to bite the youngest of the children from upstairs. I was gnawing on a bone and he took it away. A bone for a bone, I thought, and bit him in the leg.

But the master and the mistress put all the blame on me. And ever since then I have been chained. The dampness has spoiled my voice. Can't you hear how hoarse I am? . . . Out! Out! Get out! . . . And that is the end of my story."

The snowman, who had stopped listening to the watchdog, was staring with longing through the cellar window into the housekeeper's room, where the stove stood on its four black legs. "She is exactly the same height as I am," he thought.

"It creaks so strangely inside of me," the snowman muttered. "Shall I never be able to go down into the cellar and be in the same room with her? Isn't it an innocent wish, and shouldn't innocent wishes be granted? It is my greatest, my most earnest, my only wish! And it would be a terrible injustice if it were never fulfilled! I shall get in, even if I have to break the window to do it."

"You will never get down into the cellar," the old dog said. "And if you did manage it, then the stove would make sure that you were out in a minute. . . . Out! Out!"

"I am almost out already!" cried the snowman. "I feel as if I were about to break in two."

All day long the snowman gazed through the window. In the evening the housekeeper's room seemed even more inviting. The light from the stove was so soft. It was not like the moonlight or the sunlight. "Only a stove can glow like that," he thought. Every so often, when the top door of the stove was opened to put more wood in, the bright flames would shoot out, and the blaze would reflect through the window and make the snowman blush from the neck up.

"It's more than I can bear!" he exclaimed. "See how beautiful she is when she sticks out her tongue."

•••

The night was long, but not for the snowman, who was daydreaming happily. Besides, it was so cold that everything seemed to tingle.

In the morning the cellar window was frozen; the most beautiful white flowers decorated the glass, which the snowman did not appreciate because they hid the stove from his view. It was so cold that the windows couldn't thaw and the running hose on the water pump in the yard grew an icicle. It was just the kind of weather to put a snowman in the best of moods, but it didn't. Why, it was almost a duty to be content with weather like that; but he wasn't. He was miserable. He was suffering from "stove-yearning."

"That is a very serious disease, especially for a snowman to get." The old watchdog shook his head. "I have suffered from it myself, but I got over it. . . . Out! Out! Get out! . . . I have a feeling that the weather is going to change."

And it did. It became warmer and the snowman became smaller. He didn't say a word, not even one of complaint, and that's a very telling sign.

One morning he fell apart. His head rolled off and something that looked like the handle of a broom stuck up from where he had stood. It was what the boys had used to help hold the snowman together and make him stand upright.

"Now I understand why he longed for the stove," said the old watchdog. "That's the old poker he had inside him. No wonder. Well, now that's over. . . . Out! Out! Out!"

And soon the winter was over, and the little girls sang:

"Come, anemones, so pure and white
Come, pussy willows, so soft and light,
Come, lark and cuckoo, and sing
That in February we have spring."

And no one thought about the snowman.

ELLEN'S LION

Crockett Johnson

CONVERSATION AND SONG

Ellen sat on the footstool and looked down thoughtfully at the lion. He lay on his stomach on the floor at her feet.

"Whenever you and I have a conversation I do all the talking, don't I?" she said.

The lion remained silent.

"I never let you say a single word," Ellen said.

The lion did not say a word.

"The trouble with me is I talk too much," Ellen continued. "I haven't been very polite, I guess. I apologize."

• • •

"Oh, that's all right, Ellen," the lion said.

Ellen sprang to her feet and jumped up and down in delight.

"You talked!" she cried. "You said something!"

"It wasn't anything that important," said the lion. "And watch where you're jumping."

"It was the way you said it," said Ellen, sitting down again. "You have such a funny deep voice!"

"I think my voice sounds remarkably like yours," the lion said.

"No, it sounds very different," Ellen told him, speaking with her mouth pulled down at the corners and her chin pressed against her chest to lower her voice. "This is how you talk."

"I don't make a face like that," said the lion.

"You don't have to. Your face is always like that," Ellen said. "It's probably why you have the kind of voice you have."

The lion did not reply.

"I didn't mean to hurt your feelings," said Ellen.

"I'm nothing but a stuffed animal. I have no feelings," the lion said and, with a sniff, he became silent.

• • •

"I like your face the way it is," Ellen said, trying to think of a way to cheer him up. "And you have got a lovely deep voice. Let's sing a song."

"What song?" said the lion.

Ellen thought of a cheerful song.

"Let's sing 'Old King Cole.' "

The lion immediately began to sing.

"Old King Cole was a merry old soul—"

"Wait," Ellen said. "Let's sing it together."

"All right," said the lion.

"Old King Cole was a merry old soul—" Ellen sang, and then she stopped. "You're not singing."

"And a merry old soul was he—" sang the lion.

"—was he," sang Ellen, trying to catch up. *"He called for his pipe and he called for his bowl—"*

She realized the lion was not singing with her and she stopped again.

"And he called for his fiddlers three—" sang the lion.

• • •

"Can't we both sing at the same time?" Ellen said.

The lion considered the question.

"I don't think we can," he said. "Do you?"

"Let's talk," Ellen said. "It's easier."

"All right," said the lion.

"Think of something to talk about," Ellen said.

"All right," said the lion.

Ellen waited. After a minute or two she looked at the lion. He lay motionless on the floor.

"He thought so hard he fell asleep," she whispered as she left the playroom on tiptoe.

TWO PAIRS OF EYES

"I wish I had a drink of water," said Ellen in the middle of the night.

"Well, get one," said the lion, from the other end of the pillow.

"I'm afraid," Ellen said.

"Of what?" said the lion.

"Of things," said Ellen.

"What kind of things?" said the lion.

◆◆◆

"Frightening things," Ellen said. "Things I can't see in the dark. They always follow along behind me."

"How do you know?" said the lion. "If you can't see them—"

"I can't see them because they're always behind me," said Ellen. "When I turn around they jump behind my back."

"Do you hear them?" asked the lion.

"They never make a sound," Ellen said, shivering. "That's the worst part of it."

The lion thought for a moment.

"Hmm," he said.

"They're awful," Ellen continued.

"Ellen," the lion said, "I don't think there are any such things."

"Oh, no? Then how can they scare me?" said Ellen indignantly. "They're terribly scary things."

"They must be exceedingly scary," said the lion. "If they keep hiding in back of you they can't be very brave."

Ellen frowned at the lion. Then she considered what he had said.

"I guess they're not very brave," she agreed. "They wouldn't dare bother me if I could look both ways at the same time."

"Yes," said the lion. "But who has two pairs of eyes?"

"Two people have," Ellen said, staring up at where the ceiling was when it wasn't so dark. "I wouldn't be afraid to go down the hall for a drink of water if I was two people."

Suddenly she reached out for the lion, dragged him to her, and looked him in the eyes.

"Mine are buttons," he said. "They're sewn on. I can't see very well in the dark."

"Nobody can," Ellen whispered, as she got out of bed. "But the things don't know that."

"How do you know they don't know?" said the lion.

"I know all about them," said Ellen. "After all, I made them up in my head didn't I?"

"Ah," said the lion. "I said there were no such things."

• • •

"But of course there are," Ellen said. "I just told you I made them up myself."

"Yes," the lion said. "But—"

"So I should know, shouldn't I?" said Ellen, putting the lion up on her shoulder so that he faced behind her. "Stop arguing with me and keep your eyes open."

"They're buttons," said the lion, bouncing on Ellen's shoulder as she walked across the bedroom. "My eyes never close."

"Good," said Ellen, and she opened the door to the hall.

With a firm grip on the lion's tail to hold him in place, she marched down the hall to the

• • •

bathroom, drank a glass of water, and marched back to bed. She looked straight ahead all the way while the lion stared into the darkness behind her, and during the entire trip not a single thing dared bother either of them.

A KIND OF SILENCE

Ellen came in carrying a book with no pictures in it. As she sat down she turned to the lion on the footstool beside the big chair.

"Please be very silent," she said. "I have a book I want to read."

The lion, who had been silent anyway, became very silent.

"It bothers people who want to read, when somebody is talking all the time," Ellen explained, patting the lion on the head. "You understand that, don't you?"

The lion said nothing.

Ellen opened the book. After a moment she closed it, keeping her thumb in the page, and looked sidewise at the lion. Not a hair of his artificial fur stirred.

• • •

"You don't have to exaggerate like that," she said.

The lion continued to sit there silently.

"There are all kinds of ways of being silent," Ellen said. "Why can't you be silent in a nice way?"

The lion kept silent in the same manner, with his button eyes staring straight ahead into space.

"You're sulking," said Ellen. "Just because I want a few minutes of peace and quiet, your feelings are hurt. Tell me now, honestly, aren't you ashamed of yourself?"

The lion told her nothing.

"You're trying to annoy me," Ellen said. "But I don't care. I'm not paying the slightest attention to you."

She opened the book again and settled back in the chair. For a long time she studied the print on the first page and paid no attention to the lion. But as she turned the page she happened to glance down at him.

"My!" she said. "You're in a temper."

She put the open book on the other arm of the chair and twisted herself over the arm beside the lion. He hadn't moved. He sat rigid, staring unblinkingly at nothing.

"You've been sitting there all this time, seething with anger," said Ellen.

The lion sat there.

"You're speechless with rage, aren't you?" said Ellen.

The lion didn't speak.

"You're wishing you were a real lion, so you could bite and scratch me," said Ellen. "Don't deny it."

The lion didn't deny it.

"Well!" said Ellen. "I can't have a wild animal around that wants to bite and scratch me every time I ask him to do a simple thing like keep quiet for a few minutes."

She shook her head in dismay.

"The house will be always full of doctors and nurses, putting bandage stickers on me,"

•••

she said. "And do you know what will happen to you?"

She pointed her finger at the lion but drew it back quickly before it could be scratched or bitten.

"They'll give you rabies tests, that's what."

A new thought struck her, and her eyes widened in alarm.

"And maybe some day you'll get in such a terrible temper you won't know what you're doing," she said. "And you'll eat me all up!"

Ellen showed no surprise when the lion didn't deny even that possibility. She shook her head hopelessly and looked very sad.

"Afterwards, when you've calmed down, you'll look around for me and I won't be there," she said. "And then you'll be sorry, when it's too late."

She put on her sorriest face for the lion, but nothing would make him change his attitude. Ellen sighed.

"Won't you be sorry?" she said.

•••

But the lion continued to stare silently off into space.

"You know, the least you can do is look at me when I'm talking to you," Ellen said.

She reached down and picked up the lion, and she sat him on her lap facing her. She looked into his button eyes.

"Won't you be sorry?"

"Yes, Ellen," said the lion.

"That's better," said Ellen.

She put the lion back on the footstool.

"And you see that you've really got to learn to control your temper, don't you?" she said.

"Yes, Ellen," said the lion.

"I'm glad you realize it," Ellen said, closing the book on the arm of the chair. "What shall we do now? Can you think of any games you'd like to play?"

"I'll sit here and be silent, in a nice way," the lion said. "You go ahead and read your book."

"I don't know how to read books without pictures in them," said Ellen, giggling. "I was just pretending."

"Oh?" said the lion.

"Yes," Ellen said. "So you see? You made all that fuss over nothing at all."

Mole waggled his toes from sheer happiness.

THE RIVER BANK

Kenneth Grahame

The Mole had been working very hard all the morning, spring-cleaning his little home. First with brooms, then with dusters; then on ladders and steps and chairs, with a brush and a pail of whitewash; till he had dust in his throat and eyes, and splashes of whitewash all over his black fur, and an aching back and weary arms. Spring was moving in the air above and in the earth below and around him, penetrating even his dark and lowly little house with its spirit of divine discontent and longing.

• • •

It was small wonder, then, that he suddenly flung down his brush on the floor, said "Bother!" and "O blow!" and also "Hang spring-cleaning!" and bolted out of the house without even waiting to put on his coat. Something up above was calling him imperiously, and he made for the steep little tunnel which answered in his case to the gravelled carriage-drive owned by animals whose residences are nearer to the sun and air. So he scraped and scratched and scrabbled and scrooged, and then he scrooged again and scrabbled and scratched and scraped, working busily with his little paws and muttering to himself, "Up we go! Up we go!" till at last, pop! his snout came out into the sunlight, and he found himself rolling in the warm grass of a great meadow.

"This is fine!" he said to himself. "This is better than whitewashing!" The sunshine struck hot on his fur, soft breezes caressed his heated brow, and after the seclusion of the cellarage he had lived in so long the carol of happy birds fell on his dulled hearing almost like a shout. Jumping off all his four legs at once, in the joy of living and the delight of spring without its cleaning, he pursued

•••

his way across the meadow till he reached the hedge on the further side.

"Hold up!" said an elderly rabbit at the gap. "Sixpence for the privilege of passing by the private road!" He was bowled over in an instant by the impatient and contemptuous Mole, who trotted along the side of the hedge chaffing the other rabbits as they peeped hurriedly from their holes to see what the row was about. "Onion-sauce! Onion-sauce!" he remarked jeeringly, and was gone before they could think of a thoroughly satisfactory reply. Then they all started grumbling at each other. "How *stupid* you are! Why didn't you tell him——"

• • •

"Well, why didn't *you* say——" "You might have reminded him——" and so on, in the usual way; but, of course, it was then much too late, as is always the case.

It all seemed too good to be true. Hither and thither through the meadows he rambled busily, along the hedgerows, across the copses, finding everywhere birds building, flowers budding, leaves thrusting—everything happy, and progressive, and occupied. And instead of having an uneasy conscience pricking him and whispering "Whitewash!" he somehow could only feel how jolly it was to be the only idle dog among all these busy citizens. After all, the best part of a holiday is perhaps not so much to be resting yourself, as to see all the other fellows busy working.

He thought his happiness was complete when, as he meandered aimlessly along, suddenly he stood by the edge of a full-fed river. Never in his life had he seen a river before—this sleek, sinuous, full-bodied animal, chasing and chuckling, gripping things with a gurgle and leaving them with a laugh, to fling itself on fresh playmates that shook themselves free,

•••

and were caught and held again. All was a-shake and a-shiver—glints and gleams and sparkles, rustle and swirl, chatter and bubble. The Mole was bewitched, entranced, fascinated. By the side of the river he trotted as one trots, when very small, by the side of a man who holds one spellbound by exciting stories; and when tired at last, he sat on the bank, while the river still chattered on to him, a babbling procession of the best stories in the world, sent from the heart of the earth to be told at last to the insatiable sea.

As he sat on the grass and looked across the river, a dark hole in the bank opposite, just above the water's edge, caught his eye, and dreamily he fell to considering what a nice snug dwelling-place it would make for an animal with few wants and fond of a bijou riverside residence, above flood level and remote from noise and dust. As he gazed, something bright and small seemed to twinkle down in the heart of it, vanished, then twinkled once more like a tiny star. But it could hardly be a star in such an unlikely situation; and it was too glittering and small for a glow-worm. Then, as he looked, it winked at him, and so declared itself to be an eye; and a small face

•••

began gradually to grow up round it, like a frame round a picture.

A brown little face, with whiskers.

A grave round face, with the same twinkle in its eye that had first attracted his notice.

Small neat ears and thick silky hair.

It was the Water Rat!

Then the two animals stood and regarded each other cautiously.

"Hullo, Mole!" said the Water Rat.

"Hullo, Rat!" said the Mole.

"Would you like to come over?" inquired the Rat presently.

"Oh, it's all very well to *talk,*" said the Mole rather pettishly, he being new to a river and riverside life and its ways.

The Rat said nothing, but stooped and unfastened a rope and hauled on it; then lightly stepped into a little boat which the Mole had not observed. It was painted blue outside and white within, and was just the size for two animals; and the Mole's whole heart went out to it at once,

•••

even though he did not yet fully understand its uses.

The Rat sculled smartly across and made fast. Then he held up his fore-paw as the Mole stepped gingerly down. "Lean on that!" he said. "Now then, step lively!" and the Mole to his surprise and rapture found himself actually seated in the stern of a real boat.

"This has been a wonderful day!" said he, as the Rat shoved off and took to the sculls again. "Do you know, I've never been in a boat in all my life."

"What?" cried the Rat, open-mouthed. "Never been in a—you never—well, I—what have you been doing, then?"

"Is it so nice as all that?" asked the Mole shyly, though he was quite prepared to believe it as he leant back in his seat and surveyed the cushions, the oars, the row-locks, and all the fascinating fittings, and felt the boat sway lightly under him.

"Nice? It's the *only* thing," said the Water Rat solemnly, as he leant forward for his stroke. "Believe me, my young friend, there is *nothing*—absolutely nothing—half so much worth doing as simply messing about in boats. Simply messing,"

•••

he went on dreamily, "messing—about—in—boats; messing——"

"Look ahead, Rat!" cried the Mole suddenly.

It was too late. The boat struck the bank full tilt. The dreamer, the joyous oarsman, lay on his back at the bottom of the boat, his heels in the air.

"—about in boats—or *with* boats," the Rat went on composedly, picking himself up with a pleasant laugh. "In or out of 'em, it doesn't matter. Nothing seems really to matter, that's the charm of it. Whether you get away, or whether you don't; whether you arrive at your destination or whether you reach somewhere else, or whether you never get anywhere at all, you're always busy, and you never do anything in particular; and when you've done it there's always something else to do, and you can do it if you like, but you'd much better not. Look here! If you've really nothing else on hand this morning, supposing we drop down the river together, and have a long day of it?"

The Mole waggled his toes from sheer happiness, spread his chest with a sigh of full contentment, and leaned back blissfully into the soft cushions. "*What* a day I'm having!" he said. "Let us start at once!"

• • •

"Hold hard a minute, then!" said the Rat. He looped the painter through a ring in his landing-stage, climbed up into his hole above, and after a short interval reappeared staggering under a fat, wicker luncheon-basket.

"Shove that under your feet," he observed to the Mole, as he passed it down into the boat. Then he untied the painter and took the sculls again.

"What's inside it?" asked the Mole, wiggling with curiosity.

"There's cold chicken inside it," replied the Rat briefly; "coldtonguecoldhamcoldbeefpickled-gherkinssaladfrenchrollscresssandwidgespotted-meatgingerbeerlemonadesodawater——"

•••

"O stop, stop," cried the Mole in ecstasies. "This is too much!"

"Do you really think so?" inquired the Rat seriously. "It's only what I always take on these little excursions; and the other animals are always telling me that I'm a mean beast and cut it *very* fine!"

The Mole never heard a word he was saying. Absorbed in the new life he was entering upon, intoxicated with the sparkle, the ripple, the scents and the sounds and the sunlight, he trailed a paw in the water and dreamed long waking dreams. The Water Rat, like the good little fellow he was, sculled steadily on and forbore to disturb him.

"I like your clothes awfully, old chap," he remarked after some half an hour or so had passed. "I'm going to get a black velvet smoking suit myself some day, as soon as I can afford it."

"I beg your pardon," said the Mole, pulling himself together with an effort. "You must think me very rude; but all this is so new to me. So—this—is—a—River!"

"*The* River," corrected the Rat.

"And you really live by the river? What a jolly life!"

"By it and with it and on it and in it," said the Rat. "It's brother and sister to me, and aunts, and company, and food and drink, and (naturally) washing. It's my world, and I don't want any other. What it hasn't got is not worth having, and what it doesn't know is not worth knowing. Lord! the times we've had together! Whether in winter or summer, spring or autumn, it's always got its fun and its excitements. When the floods are on in February, and my cellars and basement are brimming with drink that's no good to me, and the brown water runs by my best bedroom window; or again when it all drops away and shows patches of mud that smells like plum-cake,

• • •

and the rushes and weed clog the channels, and I can potter about dry-shod over most of the bed of it and find fresh food to eat, and things careless people have dropped out of boats!"

"But isn't it a bit dull at times?" the Mole ventured to ask. "Just you and the river, and no one else to pass a word with?"

"No one else to—well, I mustn't be hard on you," said the Rat with forbearance. "You're new to it, and of course you don't know. The bank is so crowded nowadays that many people are moving away altogether. O no, it isn't what it used to be, at all. Otters, kingfishers, dabchicks, moorhens, all of them about all day long and always wanting you to *do* something—as if a fellow had no business of his own to attend to!"

"What lies over *there*?" asked the Mole, waving a paw towards a background of woodland that darkly framed the water-meadows on one side of the river.

"That? O, that's just the Wild Wood," said the Rat shortly. "We don't go there very much, we river-bankers."

"Aren't they—aren't they very *nice* people in there?" said the Mole a trifle nervously.

•••

"W-e-ll," replied the Rat, "let me see. The squirrels are all right. *And* the rabbits—some of 'em, but rabbits are a mixed lot. And then there's Badger, of course. He lives right in the heart of it; wouldn't live anywhere else, either, if you paid him to do it. Dear old Badger! Nobody interferes with *him*. They'd better not," he added significantly.

"Why, who *should* interfere with him?" asked the Mole.

"Well, of course—there—are others," explained the Rat in a hesitating sort of way. "Weasels—and stoats—and foxes—and so on. They're all right in a way—I'm very good friends with them—pass the time of day when we meet, and all that—but they break out sometimes, there's no denying it, and then—well, you can't really trust them, and that's the fact."

The Mole knew well that it is quite against animal-etiquette to dwell on possible trouble ahead, or even to allude to it; so he dropped the subject.

"And beyond the Wild Wood again?" he asked. "Where it's all blue and dim, and one sees what may be hills or perhaps they mayn't, and

•••

something like the smoke of towns, or is it only cloud-drift?"

"Beyond the Wild Wood comes the Wide World," said the Rat. "And that's something that doesn't matter, either to you or me. I've never been there, and I'm never going, nor you either, if you've got any sense at all. Don't ever refer to it again, please. Now then! Here's our backwater at last, where we're going to lunch."

Leaving the main stream, they now passed into what seemed at first sight like a little land-locked lake. Green turf sloped down to either edge, brown snaky tree-roots gleamed below the surface of the quiet water, while ahead of them the silvery shoulder and foamy tumble of a weir, arm-in-arm with a restless dripping mill-wheel, that held up in its turn a grey-gabled mill-house, filled the air with a soothing murmur of sound, dull and smothery, yet with little clear voices speaking up cheerfully out of it at intervals. It was so very beautiful that the Mole could only hold up both fore-paws and gasp, "O my! O my! O my!"

◆◆◆

The Rat brought the boat alongside the bank, made her fast, helped the still awkward Mole safely ashore, and swung out the luncheon-basket.

The Mole begged as a favour to be allowed to unpack it all by himself; and the Rat was very pleased to indulge him, and to sprawl at full length on the grass and rest, while his excited friend shook out the tablecloth and spread it, took out all the mysterious packets one by one and arranged their contents in due order, still gasping, "O my! O my!" at each fresh revelation. When all was ready, the Rat said, "Now, pitch in, old fellow!" and the Mole was indeed very glad to obey, for he had started his spring-cleaning at a very early hour that morning, as people *will* do, and had not paused for bite or sup; and he had been through a very great deal since that distant time which now seemed so many days ago.

• • •

"What are you looking at?" said the Rat presently, when the edge of their hunger was somewhat dulled, and the Mole's eyes were able to wander off the tablecloth a little.

"I am looking," said the Mole, "at a streak of bubbles that I see traveling along the surface of the water. That is a thing that strikes me as funny."

"Bubbles? Oho!" said the Rat, and chirruped cheerily in an inviting sort of way.

A broad glistening muzzle showed itself above the edge of the bank, and the Otter hauled himself out and shook the water from his coat.

"Greedy beggars!" he observed, making for the provender. "Why didn't you invite me, Ratty?"

• • •

"This was an impromptu affair," explained the Rat. "By the way—my friend Mr. Mole."

"Proud, I'm sure," said the Otter, and the two animals were friends forthwith.

"Such a rumpus everywhere!" continued the Otter. "All the world seems out on the river today. I came up this backwater to try and get a moment's peace, and then stumble upon you fellows!—At least—I beg pardon—I don't exactly mean that, you know."

There was a rustle behind them, proceeding from a hedge wherein last year's leaves still clung thick, and a stripy head, with high shoulders behind it, peered forth on them.

"Come on, old Badger," shouted the Rat.

The Badger trotted forward a pace or two; then grunted, "H'm! Company," and turned his back and disappeared from view.

"That's *just* the sort of fellow he is!" observed the disappointed Rat. "Simply hates Society! Now we shan't see any more of him today. Well, tell us *who's* out on the river?"

"Toad's out, for one," replied the Otter. "In his brand-new wager-boat; new togs, new everything!"

•••

The two animals looked at each other and laughed.

"Once, it was nothing but sailing," said the Rat. "Then he tired of that and took to punting. Nothing would please him but to punt all day and every day, and a nice mess he made of it. Last year it was house-boating, and we all had to go and stay with him in his house-boat, and pretend we liked it. He was going to spend the rest of his life in a house-boat. It's all the same whatever he takes up; he gets tired of it, and starts on something fresh."

"Such a good fellow, too," remarked the Otter reflectively. "But no stability—especially in a boat!"

• • •

From where they sat they could get a glimpse of the main stream across the island that separated them; and just then a wager-boat flashed into view, the rower—a short, stout figure—splashing badly and rolling a good deal, but working his hardest. The Rat stood up and hailed him, but Toad—for it was he—shook his head and settled sternly to his work.

"He'll be out of the boat in a minute if he rolls like that," said the Rat, sitting down again.

"Of course he will," chuckled the Otter. "Did I ever tell you that good story about Toad and the lock-keeper? It happened this way. Toad . . ."

An errant May-fly swerved unsteadily athwart the current in the intoxicated fashion affected by young bloods of May-flies seeing life. A swirl

•••

of water and a "cloop!" and the May-fly was visible no more.

Neither was the Otter.

The Mole looked down. The voice was still in his ears, but the turf whereon he had sprawled was clearly vacant. Not an Otter to be seen, as far as the distant horizon.

But again there was a streak of bubbles on the surface of the river.

The Rat hummed a tune, and the Mole recollected that animal-etiquette forbade any sort of comment on the sudden disappearance of one's friends at any moment, for any reason or no reason whatever.

"Well, well," said the Rat, "I suppose we ought to be moving. I wonder which of us had better pack the luncheon-basket?" He did not speak as if he was frightfully eager for the treat.

"O, please let me," said the Mole. So, of course, the Rat let him.

Packing the basket was not quite such pleasant work as unpacking the basket. It never is. But the Mole was bent on enjoying everything, and although just when he had got the basket packed and strapped up tightly he saw a plate staring up at him from the grass, and when the job had been done again the Rat pointed out a fork which anybody ought to have seen, and last of all, behold! the mustard pot, which he had been sitting on without knowing it—still, somehow, the thing got finished at last, without much loss of temper.

The afternoon sun was getting low as the Rat sculled gently homewards in a dreamy mood, murmuring poetry-things over to himself, and not paying much attention to Mole. But the Mole was very full of lunch, and self-satisfaction, and pride, and already quite at home in a boat (so he thought) and was getting a bit restless besides, and presently he said, “Ratty! Please, *I* want to row, now!”

The Rat shook his head with a smile. “Not yet, my young friend,” he said. “Wait till you've had a few lessons. It's not so easy as it looks.”

The Mole was quiet for a minute or two. But he began to feel more and more jealous of Rat, sculling so strongly and so easily along, and his pride began to whisper that he could do it every bit as well. He jumped up and seized the sculls so suddenly, that the Rat, who was gazing out

•••

over the water and saying more poetry-things to himself, was taken by surprise and fell backwards off his seat with his legs in the air for the second time, while the triumphant Mole took his place and grabbed the sculls with entire confidence.

"Stop it, you *silly* ass!" cried the Rat, from the bottom of the boat. "You can't do it! You'll have us over!"

The Mole flung his sculls back with a flourish, and made a great dig at the water. He missed the surface altogether, his legs flew up above his head, and he found himself lying on the top of the prostrate Rat. Greatly alarmed, he made a grab at the side of the boat, and the next moment—Sploosh!

Over went the boat, and he found himself struggling in the river.

O my, how cold the water was, and O, how *very* wet it felt. How it sang in his ears as he went down, down, down! How bright and welcome the sun looked as he rose to the surface coughing and spluttering! How black was his despair when he felt himself sinking again! Then a firm paw gripped him by the back of his neck. It was the

•••

Rat, and he was evidently laughing—the Mole could *feel* him laughing, right down his arm and through his paw, and so into his—the Mole's—neck.

The Rat got hold of a scull and shoved it under the Mole's arm; then he did the same by the other side of him and, swimming behind, propelled the helpless animal to shore, hauled him out, and set him down on the bank, a squashy, pulpy lump of misery.

When the Rat had rubbed him down a bit, and wrung some of the wet out of him, he said, "Now, then, old fellow! Trot up and down the towing-path as hard as you can, till you're warm and dry again, while I dive for the luncheon-basket."

•••

So the dismal Mole, wet without and ashamed within, trotted about till he was fairly dry, while the Rat plunged into the water again, recovered the boat, righted her and made her fast, fetched his floating property to shore by degrees, and finally dived successfully for the luncheon-basket and struggled to land with it.

When all was ready for a start once more, the Mole, limp and dejected, took his seat in the stern of the boat; and as they set off, he said in a low voice, broken with emotion, "Ratty, my generous friend! I am very sorry indeed for my foolish and ungrateful conduct. My heart quite fails me when I think how I might have lost that beautiful luncheon-basket. Indeed, I have been a complete ass, and I know it. Will you overlook it this once and forgive me, and let things go on as before?"

"That's all right, bless you!" responded the Rat cheerily. "What's a little wet to a Water Rat? I'm more in the water than out of it most days. Don't you think any more about it; and, look here! I really think you had better come and stop with me for a little time. It's very plain and rough, you know—not like Toad's house at all—but you haven't seen that yet; still, I can make

•••

you comfortable. And I'll teach you to row, and to swim, and you'll soon be as handy on the water as any of us."

The Mole was so touched by his kind manner of speaking that he could find no voice to answer him; and he had to brush away a tear or two with the back of his paw. But the Rat kindly looked in another direction, and presently the Mole's spirits revived again, and he was even able to give some straight back-talk to a couple of moorhens who were sniggering to each other about his bedraggled appearance.

When they got home, the Rat made a bright fire in the parlour, and planted the Mole in an armchair in front of it, having fetched down a dressing-gown and slippers for him, and told him river stories till suppertime. Very thrilling stories they were, too, to an earth-dwelling animal like Mole. Stories about weirs, and sudden floods, and leaping pike, and steamers that flung hard bottles—at least bottles were certainly flung, and *from* steamers, so presumably *by* them; and about herons, and how particular they were whom they spoke to; and about adventures down drains, and night-fishings with Otter, or excursions far

afield with Badger. Supper was a most cheerful meal; but very shortly afterwards a terribly sleepy Mole had to be escorted upstairs by his considerate host, to the best bedroom, where he soon laid his head on his pillow in great peace and contentment, knowing that his new-found friend the River was lapping the sill of his window.

This day was only the first of many similar ones for the emancipated Mole, each of them longer and fuller of interest as the ripening summer moved onward. He learnt to swim and to row, and entered into the joy of running water; and with his ear to the reed-stems he caught, at intervals, something of what the wind went whispering so constantly among them.

They saw a gipsy caravan, shining with newness.

The Open Road

Kenneth Grahame

"Ratty," said the Mole suddenly, one bright summer morning, "if you please, I want to ask you a favour."

The Rat was sitting on the river bank, singing a little song. He had just composed it himself, so he was very taken up with it, and would not pay proper attention to Mole or anything else. Since early morning he had been swimming in the river in company with his friends the ducks. And when the ducks stood on their heads suddenly, as ducks will, he would dive down and tickle their necks just under where their chins would be if ducks had chins, till they were forced to come to the surface again in a hurry, spluttering and angry and shaking their feathers at him, for it is impossible to say quite *all* you feel when your head is under water. At last they implored him to go away and attend to his own affairs and leave them to mind theirs. So the Rat went away, and sat on the river bank in the sun, and made up a song about them, which he called:

DUCKS' DITTY

All along the backwater,
Through the rushes tall,
Ducks are a-dabbling,
Up tails all!

Ducks' tails, drakes' tails,
Yellow feet a-quiver,
Yellow bills all out of sight
Busy in the river!

Slushy green undergrowth
Where the roach swim—
Here we keep our larder,
Cool and full and dim.

•••

Every one for what he likes!
We like to be
Heads down, tails up,
Dabbling free!

High in the blue above
Swifts whirl and call—
We are down a-dabbling
Up tails all!

"I don't know that I think so *very* much of that little song, Rat," observed the Mole cautiously. He was no poet himself and didn't care who knew it; and he had a candid nature.

"Nor don't the ducks neither," replied the Rat cheerfully. "They say, '*Why* can't fellows be allowed to do what they like *when* they like and *as* they like, instead of other fellows sitting on banks and watching them all the time and making remarks and poetry and things about them? What *nonsense* it all is!' That's what the ducks say."

"So it is, so it is," said the Mole, with great heartiness.

"No, it isn't!" cried the Rat indignantly.

• • •

"Well then, it isn't, it isn't," replied the Mole soothingly. "But what I wanted to ask you was, won't you take me to call on Mr. Toad? I've heard so much about him, and I do so want to make his acquaintance."

"Why, certainly," said the good-natured Rat, jumping to his feet and dismissing poetry from his mind for the day. "Get the boat out, and we'll paddle up there at once. It's never the wrong time to call on Toad. Early or late he's always the same fellow. Always good-tempered, always glad to see you, always sorry when you go!"

"He must be a very nice animal," observed the Mole, as he got into the boat and took the sculls, while the Rat settled himself comfortably in the stern.

"He is indeed the best of animals," replied Rat. "So simple, so good-natured, and so affectionate. Perhaps he's not very clever—we can't all be geniuses; and it may be that he is both boastful and conceited. But he has got some great qualities, has Toady."

Rounding a bend in the river, they came in sight of a handsome, dignified old house of mellowed red brick, with well-kept lawns reaching down to the water's edge.

"There's Toad Hall," said the Rat, "and that creek on the left, where the notice-board says, 'Private. No landing allowed,' leads to his boathouse, where we'll leave the boat. The stables are over there to the right. That's the banqueting-hall you're looking at now—very old, that is. Toad is rather rich, you know, and this is really one of the nicest houses in these parts, though we never admit as much to Toad."

They glided up the creek, and the Mole shipped his sculls as they passed into the shadow of a large boathouse. Here they saw many handsome boats, slung from the cross-beams or hauled up on a slip, but none in the water; and the place had an unused and a deserted air.

•••

The Rat looked around him. "I understand," said he. "Boating is played out. He's tired of it, and done with it. I wonder what new fad he has taken up now? Come along and let's look him up. We shall hear all about it quite soon enough."

They disembarked, and strolled across the gay flower-decked lawns in search of Toad, whom they presently happened upon resting in a wicker garden-chair, with a preoccupied expression of face, and a large map spread out on his knees.

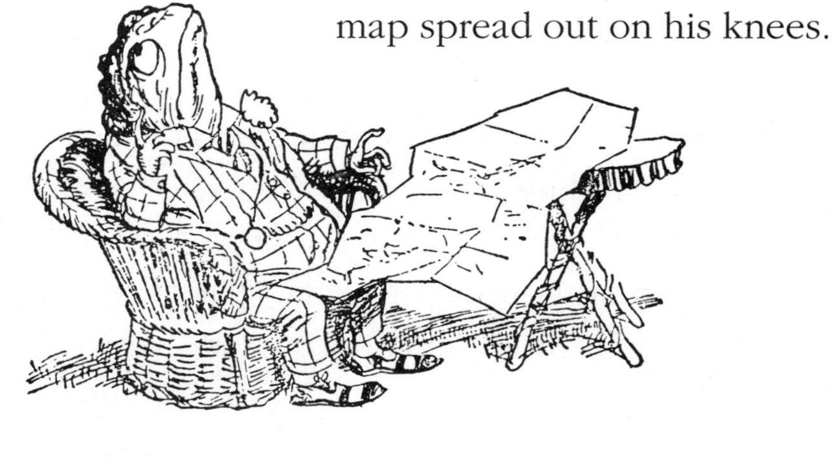

"Hooray!" he cried, jumping up on seeing them, "this is splendid!" He shook the paws of both of them warmly, never waiting for an introduction to the Mole. "How *kind* of you!" he went on, dancing around them. "I was just going to send a boat down the river for you, Ratty, with strict orders that you were to be fetched up here at once, whatever you were doing. I want you badly—both of you. Now what will you take? Come inside and have something! You don't know how lucky it is, your turning up just now!"

"Let's sit quiet a bit, Toady!" said the Rat, throwing himself into an easy chair, while the Mole took another by the side of him and made some civil remark about Toad's "delightful residence."

"Finest house on the whole river," cried Toad boisterously. "Or anywhere else, for that matter," he could not help adding.

Here the Rat nudged the Mole. Unfortunately the Toad saw him do it, and turned very red. There was a moment's painful silence. Then Toad burst out laughing. "All right, Ratty," he said. "It's only my way, you know. And it's not such a very bad house, is it? You know you rather like it yourself. Now, look here. Let's be sensible. You are the very animals I wanted. You've got to help me. It's most important!"

"It's about your rowing, I suppose," said the Rat, with an innocent air. "You're getting on fairly well, though you splash a good bit still. With a

•••

great deal of patience, and any quantity of coaching, you may——"

"O, pooh! boating!" interrupted the Toad, in great disgust. "Silly boyish amusement. I've given that up *long* ago. Sheer waste of time, that's what it is. It makes me downright sorry to see you fellows, who ought to know better, spending all your energies in that aimless manner. No, I've discovered the real thing, the only genuine occupation for a lifetime. I propose to devote the remainder of mine to it, and can only regret the wasted years, that lie behind me, squandered in trivialities. Come with me, dear Ratty, and your amiable friend also, if he will be so very good, just as far as the stable-yard, and you shall see what you shall see!"

He led the way to the stable-yard accordingly, the Rat following with a most mistrustful expression; and there, drawn out of the coach-house into the open, they saw a gipsy caravan, shining with newness, painted a canary-yellow picked out with green, and red wheels.

"There you are!" cried the Toad, straddling and expanding himself. "There's real life for you, embodied in that little cart. The open road, the dusty highway, the heath, the common, the hedgerows, the rolling downs! Camps, villages, towns, cities! Here today, up and off to somewhere else tomorrow! Travel, change, interest, excitement! The whole world before you, and a horizon that's always changing! And mind, this is the very finest cart of its sort that was ever built, without any exception. Come inside and look at the arrangements. Planned 'em all myself, I did!"

The Mole was tremendously interested and excited, and followed him eagerly up the steps and into the interiors of the caravan. The Rat only snorted and thrust his hands deep into his pockets, remaining where he was.

It was indeed very compact and comfortable. Little sleeping-bunks—a little table that folded up against the wall—a cooking-stove, lockers, bookshelves, a bird-cage with a bird in it; and pots, pans, jugs, and kettles of every size and variety.

"All complete!" said the Toad triumphantly, pulling open a locker. "You see—biscuits, potted lobster, sardines—everything you can possibly want. Soda-water here—baccy there—

• • •

letter-paper, bacon, jam, cards, and dominoes—you'll find," he continued, as they descended the steps again, "you'll find that nothing whatever has been forgotten, when we make our start this afternoon."

"I beg your pardon," said the Rat slowly, as he chewed a straw, "but did I overhear you say something about *'we,'* and *'start,'* and *'this afternoon'*?"

"Now, you dear good old Ratty," said Toad imploringly, "don't begin talking in that stiff and sniffy sort of way, because you know you've *got* to come. I can't possibly manage without you, so please consider it settled, and don't argue—it's the one thing I can't stand. You surely don't mean to stick to your dull fusty old river all your life, and just live in a hole in a bank, and *boat*? I want to show you the world! I'm going to make an *animal* of you, my boy!"

"I don't care," said the Rat doggedly. "I'm not coming, and that's flat. And I *am* going to stick to my old river, *and* live in a hole, *and* boat, as I've always done. And what's more, Mole's going to stick to me and do as I do, aren't you, Mole?"

• • •

"Of course I am," said the Mole loyally. "I'll always stick to you, Rat, and what you say is to be—has got to be. All the same, it sounds as if it might have been—well, rather fun, you know!" he added wistfully. Poor Mole! The Life Adventurous was so new a thing to him, and so thrilling; and this fresh aspect of it was so tempting; and he had fallen in love at first sight with the canary-coloured cart and all its little fitments.

The Rat saw what was passing in his mind, and wavered. He hated disappointing people, and he was fond of the Mole, and would do almost anything to oblige him. Toad was watching both of them closely.

"Come along in and have some lunch," he said diplomatically, "and we'll talk it over. We needn't decide anything in a hurry. Of course, I don't really care. I only want to give pleasure to you fellows. 'Live for others!' That's my motto in life."

During luncheon—which was excellent, of course, as everything at Toad Hall always was—the Toad simply let himself go. Disregarding the Rat, he proceeded to play upon the inexperienced Mole as on a harp. Naturally

• • •

a voluble animal, and always mastered by his imagination, he painted the prospects of the trip and the joys of the open life and the roadside in such glowing colours that the Mole could hardly sit in his chair for excitement. Somehow, it soon seemed taken for granted by all three of them that the trip was a settled thing; and the Rat, though still unconvinced in his mind, allowed his good nature to override his personal objections. He could not bear to disappoint his two friends, who were already deep in schemes and anticipations, planning out each day's separate occupation for several weeks ahead.

When they were quite ready, the now triumphant Toad led his companions to the paddock and set them to capture the old grey horse, who, without having been consulted,

•••

and to his own extreme annoyance, had been told off by Toad for the dustiest job in this dusty expedition. He frankly preferred the paddock, and took a deal of catching. Meantime Toad packed the lockers still tighter with necessaries, and hung nose-bags, nets of onions, bundles of hay, and baskets from the bottom of the cart. At last the horse was caught and harnessed, and they set off, all talking at once, each animal either trudging by the side of the cart or sitting on the shaft, as the humour took him. It was a golden afternoon. The smell of the dust they kicked up was rich and satisfying; out of thick orchards on either side the road, birds called and whistled to them cheerily; good-natured wayfarers passing them gave them "Good day," or stopped to say nice things

•••

about their beautiful cart; and rabbits, sitting at their front doors in the hedgerows, held up their fore-paws, and said, "O my! O my! O my!"

Late in the evening, tired and happy and miles from home, they drew up on a remote common far from habitations, turned the horse loose to graze, and ate their simple supper sitting on the grass by the side of the cart. Toad talked big about all he was going to do in the days to come, while stars grew fuller and larger all around them, and a yellow moon, appearing suddenly and silently from nowhere in particular, came to keep them company and listen to their talk. At last they turned into their little bunks in the cart; and Toad, kicking out his legs, sleepily said, "Well, good night, you fellows! This is the real life for a gentleman! Talk about your old river!"

"I *don't* talk about my river," replied the patient Rat. "You *know* I don't, Toad. But I *think* about it," he added pathetically, in a lower tone. "I think about it—all the time!"

The Mole reached out from under his blanket, felt for the Rat's paw in the darkness, and gave it a squeeze. "I'll do whatever you like, Ratty," he whispered. "Shall we run away tomorrow

• • •

morning, quite early—*very* early—and go back to our dear old hole on the river?"

"No, no, we'll see it out," whispered back the Rat. "Thanks awfully, but I ought to stick by Toad till this trip is ended. It wouldn't be safe for him to be left to himself. It won't take very long. His fads never do. Good night!"

The end was indeed nearer than even the Rat suspected.

After so much open air and excitement the Toad slept very soundly, and no amount of shaking could rouse him out of bed next morning. So the Mole and Rat turned to, quietly and manfully, and while the Rat saw to the horse, and lit a fire, and cleaned last night's cups and platters, and got things ready for breakfast, the Mole trudged off to the nearest village, a long way off, for milk and eggs and various necessaries the Toad had, of course, forgotten to provide. The hard work had all been done, and the two animals were resting, thoroughly exhausted, by the time Toad appeared on the scene, fresh and gay, remarking what a pleasant easy life it was they were all leading now, after the cares and worries and fatigues of housekeeping at home.

• • •

They had a pleasant ramble that day over grassy downs and along narrow by-lanes, and camped, as before, on a common, only this time the two guests took care that Toad should do his fair share of the work. In consequence, when the time came for starting next morning, Toad was by no means so rapturous about the simplicity of the primitive life, and indeed attempted to resume his place in his bunk, whence he was hauled by force. Their way lay, as before, across country by narrow lanes, and it was not till the afternoon that they came out on the high road, their first high road; and there disaster, fleet and unforeseen, sprang out on them—disaster momentous indeed to their expedition, but simply overwhelming in its effect on the after-career of Toad.

They were strolling along the high road easily, the Mole by the horse's head, talking to him, since the horse had complained that he was being frightfully left out of it, and nobody considered him in the least; the Toad and the Water Rat walking behind the cart talking together—at least Toad was talking, and Rat was saying at intervals, "Yes, precisely; and what did *you* say to *him*?"—and thinking all the time of something very different, when far behind them they heard a faint warning hum, like the drone of a distant bee. Glancing back, they saw a small cloud of dust, with a dark centre of energy, advancing on them at incredible speed, while from out the dust a faint "Poop-poop!" wailed like an uneasy animal in pain. Hardly regarding it, they turned to resume their conversation, when in an instant (as it seemed) the peaceful scene was changed, and with a blast of wind and a whirl of sound that made them jump for the nearest ditch, it was on them! The "poop-poop" rang with a brazen shout in their ears, they had a moment's glimpse of an interior of glittering plate-glass and rich morocco, and the magnificent motor-car, immense, breath-snatching, passionate, with its pilot tense and hugging his wheel, possessed all earth and air for the fraction of a second, flung an enveloping cloud of dust that blinded and enwrapped them utterly, and then dwindled to a speck in the far distance, changed back into a droning bee once more.

The old grey horse, dreaming, as he plodded along, of his quiet paddock, in a new raw situation such as this simply abandoned himself to his natural emotions. Rearing, plunging,

backing steadily, in spite of all the Mole's efforts at his head, and all the Mole's lively language directed at his better feelings, he drove the cart backwards towards the deep ditch at the side of the road. It wavered an instant—then there was a heart-rending crash—and the canary-coloured cart, their pride and their joy, lay on its side in the ditch, an irredeemable wreck.

The Rat danced up and down in the road, simply transported with passion. "You villains!" he shouted, shaking both fists. "You scoundrels, you highwaymen, you—you—road-hogs! I'll have the law of you! I'll report you! I'll take you through all the Courts!" His homesickness had quite slipped away from him, and for the moment he was the skipper of the canary-coloured vessel driven on a shoal by the reckless jockeying of rival mariners, and he was trying to recollect all the fine and biting things he used to say to masters of steam-launches when their wash, as they drove too near the bank, used to flood his parlour carpet at home.

•••

Toad sat straight down in the middle of the dusty road, his legs stretched out before him, and stared fixedly in the direction of the disappearing motor-car. He breathed short, his face wore a placid, satisfied expression, and at intervals he faintly murmured "Poop-poop!"

The Mole was busy trying to quiet the horse, which he succeeded in doing after a time. Then he went to look at the cart, on its side in the ditch. It was indeed a sorry sight. Panels and windows smashed, axles hopelessly bent, one wheel off, sardine-tins scattered over the wide world, and the bird in the bird-cage sobbing pitifully and calling to be let out.

The Rat came to help him, but their united efforts were not sufficient to right the cart. "Hi! Toad!" they cried. "Come and bear a hand, can't you!"

The Toad never answered a word, or budged from his seat in the road, so they went to see what was the matter with him. They found him in a sort of trance, a happy smile on his face, his eyes still fixed on the dusty wake of their destroyer. At intervals he was still heard to murmur "Poop-poop!"

• • •

The Rat shook him by the shoulder. "Are you coming to help us, Toad?" he demanded sternly.

"Glorious, stirring sight!" murmured Toad, never offering to move. "The poetry of motion! The *real* way to travel! The *only* way to travel! Here today—in next week tomorrow! Villages skipped, towns and cities jumped—always somebody else's horizon! O bliss! O poop-poop! O my! O my!"

"O *stop* being an ass, Toad!" cried the Mole despairingly.

"And to think I never *knew*!" went on the Toad in a dreamy monotone. "All those wasted years that lie behind me, I never knew, never even *dreamt*! But *now*—but now that I know, now that I fully realize! O what a flowery track lies spread before me, henceforth! What dust-clouds shall spring up behind me as I speed on my reckless way! What carts I shall fling carelessly into the ditch in the wake of my magnificent onset! Horrid little carts—common carts—canary-coloured carts!"

"What are we to do with him?" asked the Mole of the Water Rat.

•••

"Nothing at all," replied the Rat firmly. "Because there is really nothing to be done. You see, I know him from old. He is now possessed. He has got a new craze, and it always takes him that way, in its first stage. He'll continue like that for days now, like an animal walking in a happy dream, quite useless for all practical purposes. Never mind him. Let's go and see what there is to be done about the cart."

A careful inspection showed them that, even if they succeeded in righting it by themselves, the cart would travel no longer. The axles were in a hopeless state, and the missing wheel was shattered into pieces.

The Rat knotted the horse's reins over his back and took him by the head, carrying the bird-cage and its hysterical occupant in the other hand. "Come on!" he said grimly to the Mole. "It's five or six miles to the nearest town, and we shall just have to walk it. The sooner we make a start the better."

"But what about Toad?" asked the Mole anxiously, as they set off together. "We can't leave him here, sitting in the middle of the road by himself, in the distracted state he's in!

•••

It's not safe. Supposing another Thing were to come along?"

"O, *bother* Toad," said the Rat savagely. "I've done with him!"

They had not proceeded very far on their way, however, when there was a pattering of feet behind them, and Toad caught them up and thrust a paw inside the elbow of each of them; still breathing short and staring into vacancy.

"Now, look here, Toad!" said the Rat sharply, "as soon as we get to the town, you'll have to go straight to the police-station, and see if they know anything about that motor-car and who it belongs to, and lodge a complaint against it. And then you'll have to go to a blacksmith's or a wheelwright's and arrange for the cart to be fetched and mended and put to rights. It'll take time, but it's not quite a hopeless smash. Meanwhile, the Mole and I will go to an inn and find comfortable rooms where we can stay till the cart's ready, and till your nerves have recovered their shock."

"Police-station! Complaint!" murmured Toad dreamily. "Me *complain* of that beautiful, that heavenly vision that has been vouchsafed me!

•••

Mend the *cart!* I've done with carts forever. I never want to see the cart, or to hear of it, again. O, Ratty! You can't think how obliged I am to you for consenting to come on this trip! I wouldn't have gone without you, and then I might never have seen that—that swan, that sunbeam, that thunderbolt! I might never have heard that entrancing sound, or smelt that bewitching smell! I owe it all to you, my best of friends!"

The Rat turned from him in despair. "You see what it is?" he said to the Mole, addressing him across Toad's head. "He's quite hopeless. I give it up—when we get to the town we'll go to the railway-station, and with luck we may pick up a train there that'll get us back to River Bank tonight. And if ever you catch me going a-pleasuring with this provoking animal again!" He snorted, and during the rest of that weary trudge addressed his remarks exclusively to Mole.

•••

On reaching the town they went straight to the station and deposited Toad in the second-class waiting-room, giving a porter twopence to keep a strict eye on him. They then left the horse at an inn stable, and gave what directions they could about the cart and its contents. Eventually, a slow train having landed them at a station not very far from Toad Hall, they escorted the spell-bound, sleep-walking Toad to his door, put him inside it, and instructed his housekeeper to feed him, undress him, and put him to bed. Then they got out their boat from the boathouse, sculled down the river home, and at a very late hour sat down to supper in their own cosy riverside parlour, to the Rat's great joy and contentment.

The following evening the Mole, who had risen late and taken things very easy all day, was sitting on the bank fishing, when the Rat, who had been looking up his friends and gossiping, came strolling along to find him. "Heard the news?" he said. "There's nothing else being talked about, all along the river bank. Toad went up to Town by an early train this morning. And he has ordered a large and very expensive motor-car."

ACKNOWLEDGMENTS

All possible care has been taken to trace ownership and secure permission for each selection in this series. The Great Books Foundation wishes to thank the following authors, publishers, and representatives for permission to reprint copyrighted material:

THE BLACK HEART OF INDRI, by Dorothy Hoge. Copyright 1966 by Dorothy Hoge. Reprinted by permission of Charles Scribner's Sons, an imprint of Macmillan Publishing Company.

THE GREEN MAN, by Gail E. Haley. Copyright 1979 by Gail E. Haley. Reprinted by permission of the author.

THE MOUSEWIFE, by Rumer Godden. Copyright 1951, 1979 by Rumer Godden. Reprinted by permission of Viking Penguin, Inc.

The Fire on the Mountain, from THE FIRE ON THE MOUNTAIN AND OTHER ETHIOPIAN STORIES, by Harold Courlander and Wolf Leslau. Copyright 1950 by Holt, Rinehart and Winston, Inc.; renewed 1978 by Harold Courlander, Wolf Leslau, and Robert W. Kane. Reprinted by permission of Harold Courlander.

The Man Whose Trade Was Tricks, from YES AND NO STORIES, by George and Helen Papashvily. Copyright 1946, 1974 by George and Helen Papashvily. Reprinted by permission of HarperCollins Publishers.

How the Tortoise Became, from HOW THE WHALE BECAME AND OTHER STORIES, by Ted Hughes. Copyright 1963 by Ted Hughes. Reprinted by permission of Faber and Faber Limited.

Tom-Tit-Tot, from ENGLISH FAIRY TALES, by Flora Annie Steel. Copyright 1918 by Macmillan Publishing Company; renewed 1946 by Mabel H. Webster. Reprinted by permission of Macmillan Publishing Company.

The Snowman, from THE COMPLETE FAIRY TALES AND STORIES, by Hans Christian Andersen. Copyright 1974 by Eric Christian Haugaard. Reprinted by permission of Doubleday, a division of Bantam, Doubleday, Dell Publishing Group, Inc.

Conversation and Song and *Two Pairs of Eyes,* from ELLEN'S LION, by Crockett Johnson. Copyright 1959 by Crockett Johnson. *A Kind of Silence,* from THE LION'S OWN STORY, by Crockett Johnson. Copyright 1963 by Crockett Johnson. Published by Harper & Row, Publishers, Inc. Reprinted by permission of Ruth Krauss.

ILLUSTRATION CREDITS

Brock Cole prepared the illustrations for *The Green Man, Woman's Wit,* and *How the Tortoise Became.*

Donna Diamond prepared the illustrations for *The Mousewife.*

Leo and Diane Dillon prepared the illustrations for *The Fire on the Mountain.*

Frank Gargiulo prepared the illustrations for *The Man Whose Trade Was Tricks.*

Emily Arnold McCully prepared the illustrations for *The Snowman.*

Ernest Shepard's illustrations for *The River Bank* and *The Open Road* are from THE WIND IN THE WILLOWS, by Kenneth Grahame.

Ed Young prepared the illustrations for *The Black Heart of Indri, Tom-Tit-Tot,* and *Ellen's Lion.*

Cover art by Ed Young.

Text and cover design by William Seabright, William Seabright & Associates.